She's not your average teenager…She starts fires with her mind!

Sixteen-year-old Sable Mosley thinks her life is over when her parents send her to a psychiatric hospital, but that's only the beginning. She's isn't the only person there who has freaky powers. There is a whole race of people classified by the government as The Diseased—they can see the future, create air shields, or even drain the life out of others.

Then she escapes with the breathtakingly-handsome Brandon Harper, and her very existence is threatened. A secret government agency is hunting down people like Brandon, and now Sable, determined to turn them into biological weapons or kill them. Can Sable survive her attraction to Brandon, her new life as an enemy of the state, *and* the government assassins, or will she forfeit everything for just being who she is?

We wanted to cause a scene, but we got a little more that we bargained for...

Brandon shook his head, the action stiff. "Sable, look at your hands."

"There's nothing wrong with my—" As I held my hands up to examine them, I realized why the woman screamed and why Brandon's shocked expression was still glued on his face. Bright green flames licked across my skin. I looked myself up and down. The flames were everywhere. Even my hair was on fire, but nothing burned. It was like a soft aura of fire. My eyes frantically darted over Brandon, making sure he wasn't burned. Everything about him was intact. Then the accusations of the growing crowd around us began assaulting my ears.

"Is she a witch?" a child asked.

"She's one of those Diseased, like they talked about on the news," a man said.

"The boy must be, too. Look, he's unharmed," another man noted.

"What do we do with them?" a woman inquired.

All the overlapping conversations buzzed in my head like angry hornets trapped in a mason jar. I resisted the urge to press my hands tightly over my ears. In slow movements, Brandon made his way over to stand beside me. I was vaguely aware of some of the men loading and cocking their hunting rifles.

"Now we fight," Brandon murmured.

Then a blast of electric currents shattered the streetlights, casting a harsh bluish white light in their wake. Screams and cries of fear rang out into the night. Gunshots exploded above the chaos. I stood stunned in the middle of it all, watching everything as if it happened in slow motion.

"Sable!" Brandon's voice sounded very far away, even though he stood right in front of me. He got farther and farther away from me as my vision tunneled in on his panic-stricken face, then it faded to black all together. All the while, I burned. It was for him, I realized. Burning from the inside out until everything was gone.

KUDOS for *The Diseased*

I thought The Diseased by Marissa Bauder was terrific. Sable Mosley has abilities. But not like other 16 year olds. When Sable gets angry, things catch on fire. Now she's in an institution for crazies. Her parents think it's for her own good. Little do they know that in the basement is where they keep "the screamers." The nurse said "some of the patients were more 'volatile' then others," a chilling thought since most of the patients all looked pretty volatile to Sable…But just as Sable thinks her life is about to end, she finds she has an unexpected ally with some secrets of his own, including the mysterious Mr. Shaw. The book is a real page-turner. – *Taylor Jones, reviewer*

The Diseased by Marissa Bauder is a classic paranormal thriller with a twist. It revolves around Sable Mosley, a teenager who can start fires with her mind. Reminds me of a movie I saw long ago called *Carrie* about another girl who could start fires with her mind. However, in Sable's case there are a whole bunch of kids who have unique abilities. The government calls them The Diseased. The characters are well developed, the action fast and heavy, the plot solid and strong. There are enough surprises, twists and turns, and unpredictable events, that it really is hard to put the book down before you get to the end. I was caught up immediately and the book held my interest until the very last page. – *Regan Murphy, reviewer*

ACKNOWLEDGEMENTS

I would like to thank everyone who has helped in giving me the opportunity to share my story with the world. A huge thank you goes out to Janelle, who was my editor before I had a publisher. Thanks to Travis, who helped me realize I do indeed have a male audience. To Cassie, thank you for creating such a beautiful cover for my story and creating an illustration of Sable, who I could only paint with words and draw as a stick figure. Thank you to everyone at Black Opal Books for providing an outlet for my story to reach the masses. Lastly, but certainly not least, thanks to my family and friends who have tirelessly supported me as a storyteller as soon as I could explain the complicated web of relationships between my never-ending sea of imaginary friends.

ACKNOWLEDGMENTS

THE

DISEASED

Marissa Bauder

A BLACK OPAL BOOKS PUBLICATION

GENRE: YA/PARANORMAL THRILLER/PARANORMAL ROMANCE

THE DISEASED
Copyright © 2013 by Marissa Bauder
Cover Design by Cassie Wolfe
All cover art copyright © 2013
All Rights Reserved
Print ISBN: 978-1-626940-26-0

First Publication: JUNE 2013

Published by Black Opal Books **http://www.blackopalbooks.com**

DEDICATION

For Travis, who is always enthusiastic for each new chapter, no matter how long it takes me to get it to him.

I

et go of me! I'm not crazy! Please don't do this!" I begged as two men in all white two-piece suits wrestled me into a strait jacket. My shallow gasps of breath didn't come from struggling against my restraints and my captors, although I was putting up one hell of a fight. It was out of panic. I didn't deserve to go to the nut house. The fires weren't my fault.

As my mother buried her face against my father's shoulder, he put a loving arm around her and stared at me. His steel gaze hardened his brown eyes, ones I'd always known to be so soft and caring. In a voice hollow of emotion he said to me, "It's for your own protection, Sable."

A strangled cry escaped my throat. *How did it all come to this*? My first instinct was to cry, but I would be damned if I'd show them any weakness. Or let these people, who thought I should be locked in a nut house, see that their betrayal broke me up inside. No freaking way.

I screamed as loud as I could and thrashed as hard as I could. But the men in white still dragged me out of my home and into the back of their van. That would be a show my neighbors wouldn't soon forget.

The back of the van looked just like the prison vans in the movies. A bench lined three walls of the chamber, with a slab of bulletproof glass separating the cab from the prisoners. Above the benches were hooks anchored into the walls. Before I had enough time to wonder what those were for, I found out—they clipped the back of my strait jacket to it. That didn't stop me from stomping my feet and screaming the whole way there. The men pointedly ignored my rampage.

Since I was sitting on the wall on the left, I could see a little out of the windshield. The van pulled up to a pair of wrought iron gates that had to be at least fifteen feet high. I heard a code being punched into a keypad, which was followed by a low whistling noise and the subsequent sound of the gates scraping across the gravel driveway.

A few minutes later, the van stopped again, but this time, the engine was turned off. The men opened the doors and released the chain connecting me to the van's wall, making sure I wouldn't have a chance to run.

When they herded me around the side of the van, I stood before a building that mimicked the cinematic depiction of everything a nut house promised to be. The wrought iron gates had tipped me off about what I was to expect once I could fully see my impending prison.

Weathered brick with crumbling mortar housed The Geraldine S. Cannon Hospital for the Mentally Disturbed, more commonly known as the "Crazy Cannon Place." The thick haze of smog in the air told me that I'd arrived in New York and was no longer in my home state of Connecticut. The Crazy Cannon Place was on a spit of man-made island off the coast of New York. It was far enough away from civilization so that if someone escaped, they wouldn't have much chance making it back to the normal people. A quick glance over my shoulder brought the barbed wire fence surrounding the property into focus. This place was getting more and more clichéd by the minute.

A plump woman, with brown hair streaked gray at her temples, waited at the metal double-door entrance for us with a wheelchair. I was freed from the straight jacket only to be strapped into the wheelchair, buckled in at my waist, wrists, and ankles.

"We'll take good care of you here," she promised me as she wheeled me into the lobby.

The walls were painted stark white and pictures of different flowers hung on them. The frames were plastic, and I assumed that the protective clear plate covering the pictures were plastic, too, not glass.

A few plastic chairs, which were bolted to the walls, littered the space. The plump woman wheeled me over to the desk, where a waif of a woman typed furiously on her computer. Her fingers flew over the keys, hazel eyes peering over the tops of her thin wire framed glasses.

"Name?" she asked briskly. She was all business, whereas the woman wheeling me around seemed sorry for me that I was here.

I wasn't going to answer her, but the plump woman did for me. "Sable Mosley."

"Age?"

"Sixteen," the nurse—at least, I assumed she was a nurse—responded.

"Ailment?"

"Hallucinations," the nurse informed her.

"Hallucinations?" I asked incredulously. "Are you for real? Why? Do you think I'm insane?"

The receptionist seemed interested in the answer to my demand, too, so the nurse indulged me. She said quietly, "You think that you start fires."

"No," I corrected her, "My parents think I start fires." The word *parents* left a bad taste in my mouth, considering they'd just fed me to the lions, so to speak.

"There are tons of kids who consider themselves pyromaniacs. Why is this girl an exception?" the receptionist asked, finally looking up from her monitor.

"She thinks she starts fires with her mind. Using only her mind," the nurse responded.

My mouth dropped open. I'd never admit it to anyone else, but I knew I started fires. I didn't mean to, but it usually happened when I was really mad. I always tried to keep my temper in check, but when it built up too much, something always exploded into flames. It might be my neighbor's mailbox, the bathroom rug, or the oak tree in my back yard. My mom said that I was screaming about starting fires in my sleep one night about a week or so ago, but I told her it was just a nightmare. Apparently, she and my father thought otherwise. The police didn't believe that it was only nightmares, either.

The receptionist seemed satisfied with the information she'd gathered from the nurse and asked no more questions. She stared back at her computer monitor and resumed typing at her furious pace. The nurse wheeled me away from the front desk and into an elevator. I assumed I would go straight to my prison cell, but we stopped off on the second floor to rid me of my attire and the few meager possessions in the pockets of my jeans—my house keys and a tube of lip balm. In exchange I received a pair of pale yellow scrubs. Staring at the hideous attire with contempt, I watched longingly as the last traces of my old life were sealed in a plastic bag with my name on it and locked in a large metal filing cabinet. The staff were all dressed in navy blue scrubs, so I guessed that's how new people were supposed to differentiate between the patients and the employed.

After I redressed in front of a bunch of strangers, the nurse strapped me back into the wheel chair and pushed me into the elevator. At this point, the contempt left me feeling hollow and numb. It was awkward to get undressed in front of my family doctor. Being naked in front of a bunch of people treating you like a feral animal trapped in a corner was downright humiliating.

The elevator stopped on the fifth floor, the one at the very top.

"So, where do you keep the screamers?" This was my lame attempt at a joke.

"In the basement. Why, are you a screamer?" the nurse replied. Her answer caused a shiver to rake up my spine. I bit my bottom lip, a nervous response to when I felt uncomfortable.

As she wheeled me down the hall, I noticed that every door had an electronic keypad lock. Those locked rooms must have been reserved for the patients who posed the greatest risks to the others and possibly themselves. I fully expected to be shoved into a soft space with nothing flammable in it—like I could've sneaked a lighter in if I tried—because I might just be crazy enough to burn the place down. A humorless laugh escaped me. The nurse made no remark at the sound.

We stopped in front of a room numbered E6. Inwardly, I groaned at the Battleship reference that popped into my head when I read it. After the nurse quickly and discreetly punched in the code on the lock, the door clicked and she entered the room backward, pulling me with her as she went.

The room was more spacious than I'd anticipated, but everything was clinically white. The furniture in the room was sparse: a metal-framed twin sized bed, a small plastic end table painted white, and a white plastic armchair sitting next to the four-by-four-foot square window with black metal bars on the outside. A small closet was stocked with more ugly yellow scrubs and a half bathroom with a toilet and a sink was on the opposite side of the room.

The nurse unstrapped me from the wheelchair and eyed me carefully as I stood up and studied my surroundings. I unconsciously attempted to rub away the sting in my wrists where I'd been restrained for the better part of the day.

"Dinner is in an hour. A nurse will come up to escort you down to the dining hall. We're having meat loaf with stewed vegetables, and for dessert, there's lime gelatin with mixed fruit in it." Every part of that meal convinced me not to eat at this place if I could help it.

"What's your name?" I asked her.

"I'm Nurse Karen."

"What floor do you work on?"

"I generally work in the admitting and discharging department on the first floor."

"When do I get out of here?" I didn't think she'd tell me, but I had to ask anyhow.

"After Doctor Pantiel deems you cured." She turned on her heel and closed the door behind her. I heard her punching in another code and the subsequent beeping of the lock to indicate that it was armed.

For a long while, I stood in the middle of the room. How did I end up in this place? How could my parents do this to me? Well, they weren't my parents anymore. The only family I had in the world locked me in a loony bin. As I contemplated that fact, my chest constricted. I walked over to my bed in a sort of stupor and sank down onto it. A wave of loneliness washed over me, sending a single tear rushing down my cheek.

I wouldn't allow myself any more. There was no time to wallow in pity now. Even when I was with my family, I'd felt alone. I was the freak who started fires just by thinking about them.

I was twelve the first time it happened and I knew I'd done it. I was at school. It was the middle of winter, and the snowstorm the night before left the temperature beyond frigid that morning. Class wouldn't start for another twenty minutes, and my bus was always early. The wind whipped around the campus, chilling all the students to the core. Most of them laughed and gossiped with each other, but I sat alone.

As the wind lashed out in another violent blast of cold, I wished desperately for something to keep me warm. A vision popped into my head of homeless people sitting around a burning trash can, warming their tired bones. I envied them of that warmth, and before I realized what had happened, the steel trashcan a few yards away from me starting smoking.

When I peered inside, tiny flames licked at the garbage inside it. I gaped at the steadily growing fire until one of the teachers noticed the smoke and pulled the fire alarm.

Since I was the only one near the fire, I was brought inside by school officials and the principal questioned me about the cause of the fire, while my possessions were searched for lighters or matches. I answered everything innocently, and I played dumb, claiming I had no idea who or what caused the fire. Inside, my head was reeling. I wished for fire in a trashcan, and it happened.

I tested the theory later on at home. I held a piece of paper in my hand and visualized it burning. At the corner of the page, a flame yawned to life and rapidly ate up the page in my hand. There was no doubt in my mind then: I caused the fire, at school and at home, and no one could ever know.

After that I never started a fire again on purpose. I knew how dangerous fires could be if they weren't used responsibly, like burning down whole forests. That didn't stop them from finding me, though. Sometimes, if I was really angry or upset things around me would erupt into flames.

I didn't know how to stop, so I started keeping journals. I'd never believed in keeping one before. I preferred to speak my mind when I had an opinion about something. But I couldn't risk the consequences anymore.

A thought suddenly hit me—what if I started a fire here out of frustration? There clearly was nothing to write on—or with. I made a mental note to ask the nurse who escorted me to dinner to get me some paper and a pen. Besides, if the idea of this place was to heal crazy people, they wouldn't insist on their patients staying in an environment that drove them down the path of madness, would they?

The sound of the buttons on the keypad being pushed interrupted my thoughts. A nurse, different from the one who brought me to this room, appeared in the doorway. A plastic sort of smile was spread across her face, but her eyes looked like she was exhausted.

"Time for dinner, then?" I asked as she stood in the doorway. She nodded, and so I joined her. To the left of the door in the hallway was a wheelchair with straps at the wrists and ankles. With as little disgust as I could manage, I indicated the chair with a nod of my head and said, "That won't be necessary."

The nurse nodded again and held me lightly by the elbow instead. I allowed her to steer me to the elevator and eventually to the dining hall. The space reminded me of a typical high school cafeteria. Round tables with plastic chairs lined the walls of the room with bench tables in the center. Like the rest of this facility, the walls were white, but the furniture was a faded shade of avocado green. Maybe they were donated from a school when '70s decorating style became passé.

Most of the room was filled by the time I'd arrived. People sat in groups of three or four, many of them in silence. Some discussed things like colors or numbers, while others argued about the weather. In the far back corner, a girl who didn't appear too much older than me sat alone. She was absent-mindedly pushing her mixture of carrots, peas, corn, and green beans around on her plate with her fork.

The nurse let go of my elbow, so I took a few tentative steps towards the girl. When the nurse didn't protest, I broke into my normal stride.

As I reached the table, I noticed the girl was still staring at her half eaten food. A mass of frayed-looking, dark blonde hair hid her face. I cleared my throat. "Mind if I sit?"

She shrugged and held out her hand, inviting me to join her, so I took the chair across from her. We sat in silence for a few minutes before another nurse brought me a Styrofoam tray of less than appetizing food. I immediately pushed it away. That brought a snicker out of the silent girl.

"It's the same shit all the time. You better get used to it since you never know how long you'll have to stay in this place."

"How long have you been here?" I asked. I didn't expect her to answer since we didn't know each other at all.

"Since I was twelve, so that'd be six years now," she replied evenly. My chest constricted at the thought of being here more than six hours, let alone six years. "The worst of it is the testing they do to you, but that doesn't happen to everyone. Just the 'special cases.'"

I looked at the green gelatin with squares of fruit suspended in it and shuddered. Would it be too much to ask for a cheeseburger or something?

The blonde-haired girl was watching me with the slightest hint of amusement in her violet eyes. After my gaze locked with hers, she asked, "Got a name?"

"Sable Mosley," I answered. "What's yours?"

"Ophelia Reinhardt. So, what's your crime?"

I felt nervous about telling her why I was institutionalized. It didn't really matter how she would judge me, I decided, since everyone here was deemed crazy for one reason or another. I took a deep breath before responding, "I'm accused of thinking I can start fires with my mind."

"Impressive," she said as she tenderized her brick of meatloaf with the back of her fork.

"Why'd they throw you in here?"

"I see things that no one else wants to see," she said darkly.

I didn't know if I wanted her to elaborate on that or not, so I just replied with a lame, "Ah."

The sound of plastic chair legs scraping across linoleum indicated that dinner hour was over. Spots of navy dotted the sea of pale yellow as nurses herded the patients out of the dining hall and back to their rooms.

"So what floor are you on?" I asked. Not like there was any chance of me having any kind of social life at this place. Ophelia seemed to be pretty together as far as I could tell. I was locked in my room all the time, so it wasn't as if I could wander the grounds with her or something. "I'm on the fifth floor."

"My room's in the basement," she smirked as a nurse came to escort her back to her room. "Tomorrow at breakfast?"

I nodded. "Sure." Maybe she wasn't as put together as I thought.

"Miss, I'll take you back to your room now," a male orderly told me gently.

I sighed and stood up from the table. That's when I locked eyes with him. His were icy blue and seemed to crackle beneath the surface. He was quite a bit taller than me, and built, with lean muscle. Black, shaggy hair adorned his head, curling at the temples and the nape of his neck. My stomach twisted into a knot as I took him in.

Wow, was he hot! His lips twitched at the corners as I continued to gawk at him. He raked a hand through his hair, grabbed me by my elbow, and began leading me back to E6. Well, at least there was a little bit of eye candy in this place. He didn't look much older than me, either.

As I was led back to my room, I screwed up my courage. "Can I have some paper and something to write with?"

"What do you need them for?"

"So I don't go crazy in this place."

He chuckled softly and shook his head slightly. The sound made butterflies flutter in my stomach.

"How poignantly ironic of you, Miss. It seems you haven't lost your mind quite yet."

Did he believe I wasn't crazy? "So, can I?"

"I can't authorize it, but I'll have one of the higher ups ask the doctor about it."

"Thank you," I replied breathlessly. I wanted to hug him out of gratitude, but the butterflies in my stomach made me too shy. My arm twitched, determined to stay at my side.

That night, I lay awake on my too small bed—the one in my room at home was a queen size—trying to process the events of the day. This was definitely the worst Saturday ever. Before I drifted off to sleep, I said a silent prayer that breakfast in the morning wouldn't contain any grits.

II

Breakfast left me wishing for grits. The menu consisted of rubbery scrambled eggs, dry wheat toast, and a couple slices of cantaloupe. All I ate was the fruit. Ophelia joked with me about being able to bounce the eggs off the floor like a rubber ball.

"Miss Mosley, the doctor will be ready to see you after the morning meal," a pudgy nurse informed me just as I was considering throwing my eggs on the floor to test their bounce.

Ophelia grimaced, but held her tongue until the nurse was out of earshot. "So, it's your first time on the couch, huh?" she said with an edge of animosity in her voice.

"What's therapy like?"

"Therapy in the real world? They ask you a bunch of questions about your life and how you feel about it. Dr. Pantiel tries to make you understand why you're crazy and if you re-fuse his explanations…well, he'll show you the error of your ways." Ophelia's face grew dark as she spoke.

Goose bumps broke out over my skin as I was escorted to Dr. Pantiel's office. I sat in a waiting room that was completely sterile: just white walls and plastic chairs. With each minute that passed, the knot in my stomach grew tighter. Waiting was always the worst part of anything. My imagination tended to run away with me, and that usually brought me nothing but trouble.

A tall man with broad shoulders and a barrel chest, wearing khaki slacks, a white long sleeved button-up shirt, a green nautical necktie, and black loafers came out of the doctor's office holding a chart in his hand. He scanned it briefly before speaking. "Sable Mosley."

At the sound of my name, my palms started sweating and the hairs on the back of my neck stood up. I stared at the man for a few moments before I slowly got to my feet. My legs felt like lead weights as I trudged over to his office. The man pushed the door open to allow me to pass him. I stood just inside the doorway when he closed the door behind us.

This office had the most color I'd seen at this hospital. The walls were royal blue and the wood furniture was all dark walnut. A liquor chest that looked like a globe sat open next to the doctor's desk, which was a stately structure. Equally ornate bookshelves lined the wall behind the desk and were filled with thick tomes by the likes of Sigmund Freud. The carpet was beige modern shag.

A simple wooden armchair sat opposite the desk, but I didn't sit in it until I was invited to do so. He simply indicated I should sit by a nod of his head toward the chair.

Doctor Pantiel had sandy blond hair that was greying at the temples and tired-looking, analytical brown eyes. He scanned my file and looked me over before he spoke. "I am Doctor Pantiel, as you've probably guessed. Now, it says here in your file that you were admitted to us because you believe that you can start fires with your mind."

The statement was less a checking of facts than it was a challenge. The sharpness of his gaze contradicted the small smile on his lips. I stayed silent, refusing to acknowledge something that would surely deem me crazy.

"Come now, this is an open place. You are free to speak your mind without judgment," he assured me. His focus never once left my eyes. If I said I wasn't intimidated, I'd be a liar. But I had to lie to get out of here, so naturally, I denied it.

"My parents think that."

"What would cause them to believe something like that?" the doctor questioned.

"I had a nightmare and my mom came into my room because I was screaming."

"According to your file, something was on fire in your room when your mother came in. It says that you were sobbing an apology to your mother for setting your curtains ablaze." The doctor kept his eyes trained on me, searching for the thing that would make me crack.

"Wouldn't you be delirious if you woke up from a nightmare about stuff being on fire and it was actually happening when you woke up?"

Doctor Pantiel's polite smile turned into a truly amused one. "So are you saying that you should be tried for arson? The authorities had to be called in, didn't they?"

Firemen did have to be called. The only thing that burned was my room. I prayed silently for the fire not to spread, and amazingly, it didn't. I thought maybe it hadn't because I'd asked for it not to, but God was the only one who could control something like that, right?

"The fire was ruled accidental," I replied stonily. Doctor Pantiel's eyebrow arched in a show of interest.

"So did you start the fire with your mind or with a lighter?" he pressed.

"They said it was faulty wiring in an outlet under my window." I kept my voice as even as I could manage. I couldn't let him figure out my secret.

"But your parents wouldn't feel the need to institutionalize you if the fire was truly accidental," he pointed out.

"Maybe they're the crazy ones."

"Indeed," he mused before scribbling something into my chart. I decided then that it would be best to keep quiet, at least for the rest of this session. I wished there was a clock in the room so I could see how much of the hour I had left.

Doctor Pantiel watched me intently as I remained quiet for the remainder of our session. I read the titles on the spines of the books on the bookshelves as best I could. Only half of the books were printed in English.

Many of them were in Latin, some in German, some in Italian, a few in Russian, and a few others in Chinese or Japanese. After what seemed like days, the doctor finally stood from his chair and walked over to the door.

"We'll talk again next week," he said with a false smile.

I nodded stiffly and exited the office, demanding my feet not to run.

The orderly with the crackling blue eyes waited to escort me back to my room. My breath hitched when our gazes met. The corner of his mouth twitched. *Is he trying to hide a smile?* My cheeks flushed at the thought.

"Is everything all right?" he asked gently as he began leading the way to the elevator. I nodded. Instead of grabbing my elbow, like everyone else did when they led me somewhere, he took hold of my wrist. His grip was gentle but firm, with an electric undercurrent, which made me shiver. I found myself wishing he was holding my hand. My blush deepened.

Even inside the elevator, the orderly held onto my wrist. The other nurses and orderlies always broke physical contact in the elevators, at least until the doors were about to open. Curiosity burned inside me. Aside from Ophelia, there was no one here I wanted to know better—except him. *But why?* I allowed myself only one question.

"What's your name?"

He looked momentarily startled but regained his composure quickly. "Nathaniel."

As we completed the trek back to my room, I wondered if Nathaniel had any nicknames.

Once I was back in my room, I noticed a package on the side table. It was wrapped in simple brown paper with a string of twine around it. I unwrapped it carefully and practically squealed in delight when I found a composition notebook and a fountain pen with a green marble barrel. The note attached read, *Be free.*

At least I hadn't presented myself as such a nut job that a pen and paper were considered dangerous in my hands. I wondered how whoever allowed the fountain pen overlooked the possibility that I could easily turn it into a shank. But I would never ruin a beautiful pen like that. I opened the notebook and smelled the paper. The lines were college ruled, just like I preferred.

I wondered how whoever left me this gift guessed the perfect implements. For three pages, I just wrote my name over and over again in cursive. I liked the feeling of the flow of ink onto the page. My thoughts were too jumbled to write anything else at first.

Part of me wanted to write down my feelings about being thrown into a mental institution, but I didn't feel like opening that can of worms. I didn't think it would be a good idea if someone decided to read it and discovered all the things I would never dare to speak aloud. The idea of it sent chills up my spine. Instead, I settled on the idea of writing down some of my favorite song lyrics. They always seemed to express what I couldn't.

I didn't realize how much time passed until I heard the lock on my door click and the sound of someone's footsteps as they stepped from the wood floor of the hallway onto my carpeted one. I snapped the notebook shut with the pen lodged into its spine on the page I was writing on. With a sigh I asked, "Lunch time all ready?"

"Yes, Miss Mosley. Would you like to know what's being served?" the nurse asked. I began to wonder if this place had a never-ending supply of nurses and orderlies. I was escorted by a different one every time I moved from place to place. The disappointment that my escort was not Nathaniel shocked me.

"I'll just take the surprise," I replied.

From my short experience with the food here, I assumed it was probably bland and tasted like cardboard, rubber, or a mixture of the two. The nurse simply nodded as she swooped her arm towards the open door, signaling me to walk ahead of her, at least until we got to the hallway. Her grip on my elbow was kind, but firm, as she ushered me towards the dining hall.

I looked around for Ophelia, but she wasn't there. The table we'd sat at for the past two meals was empty, so I sat there. After a few minutes, an orderly placed a tray of food in front of me that consisted of a grey colored bratwurst, grey tinged sweet corn, and a stale wheat dinner roll. The dessert was vanilla pudding with banana slices in it. What was with these people putting fruit in everything?

As the last of the patients shuffled out of the room, I finally resigned myself to that fact that Ophelia was skipping out on this meal. I wished she would have given me the memo beforehand; I probably would've passed on it, too. All I ate was the pudding—after I took the bananas out of it—and pretended it was white chocolate while I did. That was a pretty thin fantasy.

After dinner, a nurse ushered me to the elevator. I heard a pained shriek coming from below us and jumped at the sound. The nurse started drilling the *up* button on the elevator impatiently.

"What the hell was that all about?" I demanded as another cry, this one sounding more agonizing, erupted through the floor.

"Some of the patients here are more…volatile…than others," the nurse said in a too casual voice that contradicted the manic stabbing of her finger on the *up* button.

When the elevator doors opened, she let out a sigh of relief and practically pushed me inside. Another cry of tortured pain pierced through the floor as the elevator doors closed. I looked sideways at the nurse and folded my arms over my chest to tell her I didn't buy her story. She didn't make eye contact with me for the rest of the walk back to my room.

The screams echoed in my ears as I sat in solitude. In an attempt to purge them from my head, I started scribbling down song lyrics, trying my best to keep them legible. When I read them after I'd settled down some, they were all lyrics about being in emotional pain.

My heart bled for whomever was screaming down there. Were they still?

I decided this most definitely wasn't a good place to be. I had to get out of here, but I didn't know how. Where would I go? And I couldn't leave my new friend behind, either. Well, she was the closest thing I had to a friend, anyhow.

A startling realization slammed into me like a freight train: Ophelia's room was in the basement. What if that was her screaming? The pitch was too high for it to be a man. The screaming rang louder in my ears as my imagination spun wildly beyond my control.

I needed something to really distract me so I could calm down and avoid the impending inferno building within me. The first idea that popped into my head was to count sheep. It was so ridiculous that I laughed aloud. In the back of my head, part of me was conceding to the idea that I wasn't all there. Despite that, I started counting sheep. I only got to fourteen before two nurses and an orderly burst through my door.

"Miss Mosley, is everything all right?" the blonde-haired nurse asked.

"Yes," I managed, though my voice sounded strained. I didn't have to try hard to look like I was clueless as to why they were there.

"You were screaming," the red-haired nurse said quietly. No wonder my voice sounded strained. Inwardly I cursed at myself.

"I think we'd better schedule you an appointment with Doctor Pantiel in the morning," the blonde nurse decided. With that, the three intruders took their leave and left me to my sheep counting.

I lay down on my bed and stared at the popcorn ceiling. I looked for patterns in the bumps and traced them in the air with my finger. At some point, sleep overtook me.

I didn't dream very often, but when I did, it wasn't pleasant. Most girls my age dreamed about boys or school dances or stuff like that. Me? I dreamed about monsters and natural disasters and abuse.

The scene was in black and white like one of those silent movies, only this had sound. I was strapped to a table like Frankenstein's monster, with doctors wearing masks surrounding me. I couldn't even begin to count how many tubes and monitors were attached to me. The doctors scribbled furiously on clipboards while one facing away from me spoke into a microphone. My pulse hammered in my throat and my breaths came in short gasps.

People surrounded me on all sides, all of them in lab coats. As I became more attuned to my surroundings, I figured out that I was a lab experiment. I was a government experiment because someone finally discovered that I truly do psychically start fires. Lesions and poke holes were scattered across my skin. My guess was that they were trying to figure out what set me off and made me burn something up.

"Subject 8196A has been under our observation for three weeks. Five days ago, she refused to eat, so we are now force feeding her through the use of a feeding tube and hydrating her intravenously," the doctor with the microphone informed the onlookers.

Somewhere in the back of my mind, the overwhelming desire to be dead gnawed at my subconscious. My thoughts in the dream were sluggish, so I guessed I was being sedated.

"If we don't find a cure for her condition within the next three weeks, the patient will have to be lobotomized and institutionalized for the remainder of her life," the doctor concluded.

Six weeks? That was all they were giving me before they turned me into a vegetable so I wasn't dangerous anymore? And who the hell said I needed fixing to begin with! My thoughts raged in my head, but the drugs and the restraints kept my limbs from moving. I so desperately wanted to run, even though I had nowhere to go.

The part of my mind that could separate the dream me from the real me latched on to the irony of my situation. No matter where I was, in my dreams or in reality, I was a caged animal. I was at the mercy of sterile people who didn't care about me as a person. I was a number, nothing more, nothing less. And that pissed me off.

And that was when the overhead sprinkler system showered ice-cold water down onto me and the fire alarm sounded.

III

The door to my room burst open and two burly orderlies rushed inside. They started to speak but stopped short. Their jaws dropped. I followed the direction of their gaping stares and choked when I saw what they were gawking at: the plastic chair in the corner of my room looked melted on the arms and it was smoldering. A wave of panic shot through me. I was sure I'd end up in the strait jacket again.

I waited for the orderlies to restrain me while they called for backup, or whatever orderlies did with dangerous patients. All they did was stare at me. They were afraid of me. Maybe they thought I'd somehow managed to stash a lighter on me when I was admitted or they truly believed I'd psychically caused the flames.

"Call the doctor," one of the orderlies hissed into a walkie-talkie.

"Is it an emergency?" a woman's disembodied voice crackled.

"Affirmative," he confirmed. When he replaced the device into its holster on his hip, he looked at his fellow orderly.

They wordlessly exchanged their ideas about what must happen now.

They escorted me outside. I went with them without putting up a fight. Even then, they gripped my forearms tightly as if I made flames come out of my hands. The last of the stragglers were being ushered outside when I was.

The crunch of tires on gravel perforated the murmurs of the confused patients. It didn't sound loud enough to be a fire truck. Instead, an impressive looking black sedan with a shiny silver jaguar hood ornament parked at the edge of the driveway. A tired and disheveled Doctor Pantiel exited the vehicle. He looked the building over, assessing if a terrible amount of damage was done.

Since the only charred furniture in my room was the chair, I could positively confirm it was a small fire. After he was satisfied with scrutinizing the building, he turned his attention to the crowd of patients. His eyes scanned each face until they fell on mine.

His expression hardened as he folded his arms over his chest. The color leeched from my face, my blood running cold.

After a few more minutes of suspended confusion, the patients were allowed to return to their rooms. The new set of orderlies who were escorting me announced that I was being taken to Doctor Pantiel's office.

A chill of fear ran up my spine, causing me to shiver. What was going to happen to me? I was sure he already knew that I was the culprit behind the fire. The question was, would he think I was a dangerous lunatic, or would he believe that I had strange psychic abilities? For some odd reason, I was praying he just thought I was crazy. That was a simpler explanation than the truth.

I sat in that hard wooden chair in his office, waiting for him to come evaluate my mental state. After what seemed like forever, Doctor Pantiel came into the office and sat down in the chair behind his desk. For a long time, he just stared at me, his eyes never moving away from mine. The intensity of it made the hairs on the back of my neck stand on end. I tried as hard as I could to keep my breathing even.

"So," he began, his voice heavy with sleep deprivation, "I give you the benefit of the doubt, and you thank me by starting a fire in my hospital."

I didn't know what to say.

When it was clear I wasn't going to give an answer, he heaved a heavy sigh and pinched the bridge of his nose between his thumb and index finger. "Look, this isn't like you're five years old and you got caught with your hand in the cookie jar before dinner. This is arson we're talking about here. Arson. That's a felony."

"Couldn't I just plead insanity and wind up in a psych ward someplace else?" I snapped. Damn me and my mouth! My plan to remain silent was ruined.

"Is that what you're after? Are you angry that your parents had you committed? Are you acting out so someone will pay attention to you? Are you seeking retribution or attention? That's it, isn't it? You're just a spoiled little girl with a sense of entitlement," he mused. There was an increasing edge to his voice as he spoke. He'd gotten up from his chair and started pacing the floor behind his desk as he deciphered the reasoning behind my behavior.

"Look, Jude,"—I'd gotten the name from his desk plate— "You don't know anything about me! And who are you to say I'm a spoiled little girl with a sense of entitlement?" My temper was definitely getting me into trouble.

Doctor Pantiel took slow, deliberate steps toward me. He leaned his face in close to mine so I could feel his hot breath with every word he hissed into my face. "We'll see. I think

I've made your stay here too comfortable, Miss Mosley. No matter, I'll put you in your proper place—in the basement."

My blood turned to ice in my veins as a malicious smile spread across his face. I'd pissed off the wrong person. Even though I didn't know anything about who was in the basement or what kind of things happened down there, I knew it was something I didn't want. I bit my tongue as I was ushered out of his office into the awaiting hands of yet another pair of orderlies.

One was just another faceless goon. The other was Nathaniel. Maybe the orderlies, and the nurses, too, were made in the basement. An odd mixture of unadulterated fear and—excitement?—warred for dominance. As they dragged me to my new prison, Nathaniel's eyes seemed to be as wide as my own. Was he afraid for me? The thought simultaneously made me melt and stopped my breathing out of sheer panic.

The environment of the basement was a stark contrast to the hospital above. Everything here was grey and dirt smudged, whereas the hospital was all white and sterile. The air in the basement was heavy and thick with humidity. I felt like I was suffocating a little more with every inhalation. The sounds of people moaning and groaning wafted through the air. Solid iron doors with small grates at eye level concealed the people behind them.

"Lucky girl, you get a roommate since none of the cells were unoccupied," the orderly on my left said as he unlocked the door to my new prison. Just before the orderlies threw me inside the cell, Nathaniel squeezed my wrist. Was that supposed to be reassuring?

Inside, I noticed that there was a small window, which was the only source of light. It was so small that a person with average sized hands would have trouble punching through it. However, *someone* had punched through it. Even though it was barely detectable, the smell of the salty sea air was a welcome one in the midst of the stench of decay.

The sound of stones scraping against each other distracted me from observing my surroundings. I turned in the direction of the noise, which increased in both speed and volume. A few meager sparks shot from the stones.

"Hey, you're kind of cute, heh, heh," said a deep voice that sounded like the speaker had gravel lodged in his throat.

"Who are you?" I asked, my tone harsher than I'd meant.

"The name's Fang."

"Fang?" I scoffed. "You can't be serious."

"It ain't the name on my birth certificate, but it's the one I use. Now make yourself useful and put some fire in your hands so I can see your pretty face."

"Wha–what makes you think I can do that?" I stammered.

"Word travels pretty quick down in these parts. I reckon Ophelia will be glad to hear you're still around."

"What, like someone was going to kill me?" I asked sarcastically.

"You could've been carted off someplace else. The good Doctor decided you were uh, useful enough to stick around." The way Fang said "the good Doctor" sounded like he swallowed something sour. "So you gonna start us a fire, Missy?"

"It's Sable, not Missy. And I don't know if I can."

"You won't know 'til you tried. Now go on."

"I don't even know where to start," I confessed. I was sure there wasn't anything to burn in here.

"Concentrate."

I squinted my eyes shut and tried to picture a fire burning in my palms. I held my hands together out in front of me with my palms face up. The more I willed the fire to ignite on my palms, the hotter they got. Fang was silent while I tried to summon the flames. After about ten minutes, my palms went cold. I let out a growl of frustration.

"This is bull—" I stopped midsentence to find a small plume of flames flickering in my palms. The sea breeze made them twist and flutter elegantly. A smile crept across my lips. I'd really done it! A shot of panic raced through my mind and I jerked my eyes toward the ceiling. There weren't any sprinkler systems to set off down here.

"Very good," Fang chuckled. "Now, let me have a decent look at you."

I held the flames closer to my face. I saw Fang stand up from the worn looking cot he was sitting on. He stopped just in front of me and held onto my wrists. Slowly, he pulled my hands upward. As he did so, I realized that really, he wanted me to see him. He'd seen me when I was thrown into the cell.

He was a tall black man, who had been incredibly muscular at one point in time, with a bald head and a barrel chest. His shoulders were broad, the muscles pulled taut against them. If he wasn't institutionalized, I'm sure he could have been a linebacker or something.

The only flaw in his physique was his face. On the left side of it, there were four wide vertical scars. A thick film covered his left eye, making the iris look pale blue and the pupil navy, indicating that the eye was blind. His right eye was a rich brown color, almost black in the dim light.

Fang smiled. The scars made his smile twist unnaturally downward on the left. "See, I knew you was a pretty thing."

"So, what are you locked up for?"

"I got some qualities that the good Doctor finds useful, too."

I understood him not wanting to talk about it. I never wanted to talk about my psychic fire power.

"Are we locked up all the time here like they are upstairs?"

"Well, Miss Sable, we don't leave our cells for meals. They get shoved through that gap under the door. The only time we're let out is when the good Doctor orders tests for us," he answered bitterly.

"What kind of tests?" My voice was almost a whisper.

"Where do you reckon all the screaming in this place comes from?"

The sound of the woman screaming earlier echoed in my ears and made goose bumps break out all over my skin.

"Depends on what the good Doctor thinks you can do." Fang shrugged. He sat back down on the cot and patted the place next to him, inviting me to sit. I did.

"Is that…is that how you, um, got the scars?" I asked sheepishly.

"Nah, the scars are how I got the name," he smiled proudly.

We sat in silence as I used the dying flames in my palms to get a better look at the room. I noticed there was only one cot. Fang seemed nice and all, but I really didn't want to share a tiny threadbare cot with a man I *did* know, let alone one I didn't.

Loud rapid pounding on the cell door jarred me from my musings. A metal tray with a pile of what looked like discolored tapioca pudding was shoved underneath the door. Just one tray. The man who pounded on the door yelled to us, "Eat up, you freak!"

"One tray, huh? You must've had an interesting talk with the good Doctor before you were sent down here," Fang chuckled.

"He said I was spoiled and had an unwarranted sense of entitlement, so I called him Jude and here I am," I explained.

That earned a big guffaw from Fang. "He's not too fond of our lot calling him anything but his proper title."

I grimaced as I stared at the weird tapioca pudding. "I'll admit it was childish."

"Well, you ain't hardly nothing but a baby anyhow," he laughed.

"I'm sixteen!" I exclaimed indignantly.

Fang let out another of those hearty laughs of his. "Like I said," he smiled as he picked the tray up off the floor.

"What is that crap?"

He shrugged. "Dinner."

"Yeah, but what is it?"

"I reckon it's better if I don't know what this slop is." He sighed. "Seems to me they didn't make you a plate. That's probably your first punishment for pissing off the good Doctor. I'll share mine with you, if you want it."

"I'll pass, thanks." The acrid stench of the stuff was already starting to make me queasy.

"This is one of the better options we get down here. There's only so long you can starve yourself, Miss Sable, before the good Doctor will decide to be rid of you."

"I'll eat tomorrow," I promised.

Too much had gone on tonight for me to even think about eating normal food, let alone this food. Then I realized that it was really late to be having dinner. In fact, dinner upstairs was hours ago. "You're just getting fed now? Is it like that all the time?"

"We get fed when the folks upstairs feel like getting around to it. No one's in a big rush," Fang explained in between bites of slop.

The fire was gone from my hands now, and the heat returned to my skin. I gingerly touched the skin of my palms to feel for blisters. There were none. I leaned back, until my head rested against the wall, and closed my eyes. After all the excitement, exhaustion was overtaking me. Fang seemed to notice and scooted onto the floor.

"You sleep on the cot, Miss Sable. I've slept on worse than a concrete floor before, and I reckon someday, I will again. You'll need your rest. Considering what favor you're in with the good Doctor, your tests tomorrow won't be pretty," he said darkly.

I had to push those thoughts out of my mind if I was going to get the slightest bit of rest. "Thanks for letting me have the cot, Fang." I yawned. Maybe it wouldn't be as hard to fall asleep as I thought.

"My pleasure, Miss Sable," he replied softly.

"You don't have to keep calling me Miss, you know," I mumbled.

"You're not much one for pleasantries, are you?" He chuckled. He patted me on the back of my hand before he lay down on the floor. I wished I had a pillow or a blanket or something to offer him to make the ground a little less hard. Unfortunately, there was only the cot.

My surroundings and the thoughts of the ominous testing, which would take place in the morning, made me feel depressed.

I needed to see Ophelia. For some reason, I still had this nagging feeling that she was the one who'd been screaming earlier. A lead weight settled into the pit of my stomach.

I ended up tossing and turning a lot before I finally settled down enough to go to sleep. All too soon, the sun would creep over the horizon, and my descent into Hell would go from scary to terrifying.

When I was upstairs, I longed to be back at home with my family before all of this fire stuff started. I longed for the normalcy that was rapidly slipping away from me. Now, I'd just give anything to be in that room on the fifth floor.

IV

The sound of fists pounding on the metal door of my cell wrenched me from sleep. The man responsible for assaulting my door yelled from the other side of it, "Get up you freaks!"

Fang grunted and rubbed the sleep from his eyes as he sat up.

"Is that a daily occurrence?" I asked.

He nodded as he stood up and stretched.

There was a hint of the dawn breaking over the horizon shining through our broken cell window. The pale light softened the sharp lines of Fang's physique.

I watched him as he worked every muscle group, one at a time, to loosen the knots caused by his poor sleeping conditions. He looked like an athlete warming up before a sporting event. I wondered if he might have been an athlete before he got locked up here.

I tilted my head from side to side and then twisted it back and forth in an attempt to get rid of the kinks in my neck. It worked a little, but the muscles were still a little stiff when I finished.

"Mosley, get out here, now!" an orderly barked as he swung the cell door open. My chest constricted as I shuffled out of the cell. Fang gave me a knowing look before the door slammed shut in his face.

The orderly grabbed me by the arm and yanked me along the corridor. Just when I was sure my arm was coming out of the socket, we stopped at the end of a line of women. I could see ahead that they were all removing their clothing. I wondered if this was part of the testing. As I swallowed a little vomit, a chill ran up my spine.

When it was my turn to get undressed, I felt extremely self-conscious. I'd never had serious issues with my body image. Sure, my breasts could have been a little bigger and my hips could have been a little fuller and a little softer, but I was generally okay with being built slender. My problem was that there were six male orderlies watching the nude women. It was demoralizing to strip in front of these men. I'd never even been naked in front of any of my ex-boyfriends.

And then there was Nathaniel. I gasped as we locked gazes for a moment. He cast his eyes down and hurriedly walked away from the scene. My nerves eased ever so slightly knowing I wouldn't be nude in front of him.

"You can do it yourself or I can do it for you," the orderly who dragged me to this line hissed in my ear. Given the options, I undressed myself.

There were at least fifteen other women standing exposed beside me. Two others were in line behind me. A sense of degradation hung in the air. Some women looked embarrassed while others looked ashamed, and still others looked disgusted. The orderlies all had a gleam of lust in their eyes.

To my horror, I caught sight of Ophelia about six women down from me. She looked emaciated, like many of the other women in line did. She must've been down in the basement for a long time. Her hips had bruises shaped like fingers on them. My heart hurt for her. I'd have to get Fang to help me communicate with her. There wasn't a way for me to now.

An orderly stood at each end of the line and worked their way to meet in the middle, pouring liquid dish soap on top of each woman's head and over their shoulders. When they were finished, they took their places in front of us again. Another of the orderlies had a garden hose with a sprayer attachment on it in his hands. This was how we were supposed to bathe, I realized in detached horror.

I learned from the other women that this was to be a quiet process. One girl who protested was kicked on the back of her knees, causing her to collapse on the floor. I didn't know if that was common practice or if they were making an example of her. I also didn't want to find out by making myself known. When the water was blasted on me, I washed where I thought were the most vital places to clean since we weren't provided with much soap.

After the orderlies grew tired of ogling our soaked naked bodies, we were allowed to redress, but we weren't able to dry off. Our threadbare scrubs had to act as our towels and our clothes. I was grateful to be shoved back into my cell.

"It'll be my turn soon," Fang grumbled. It wasn't long before he was collected.

While I waited for him to come back, I lay down on the cot and curled into a ball, tears springing to my eyes. How awful was the testing going to be when I'd just endured something so heinous? I desperately wanted to think of something else, but I couldn't. I guessed it was a good thing that I didn't know any details about what the tests were so my imagination couldn't invent terrible situations for me to stew over, but not knowing was just as disconcerting.

I didn't know how much time had passed when Fang finally returned. My hair was still damp, so it must not have been too long. His scrubs were stuck to him, just as mine had been when I was returned from the "shower." He sat on the cot by my feet and patted my calf gingerly.

"I should've just kept my mouth shut," I mumbled into my arm, which was slung across my face.

Fang sighed. "It don't matter what you did or didn't say. The good Doctor would've found a reason to send you down here any which way. All of us that's 'special' get sent down here."

"You mean, everyone that's down here has like, super powers?" I sat up and looked at him while I hugged my knees to my chest. Fang slid back on the cot and leaned up against the wall as he chuckled.

He winked. "I don't know about all that, Miss Sable, but it's all got to do with our minds."

"So we're all psychic?"

"In a way, I guess so. Whatever it is you can do, it starts subconsciously at first, then makes itself known when you need it to."

"I don't ever recall needing to set anything on fire," I mused.

"Maybe not, but you probably needed to blow off some steam. You got a lot of rage inside, right? It explodes out of you in flames instead of you just yelling or something else more docile."

"Who said I'm full of rage?"

"You didn't say you wasn't, either."

Maybe I was subconsciously holding back what I felt about certain things. I didn't know. "So if I come clean or whatever, then will I stop setting things on fire?"

"I reckon not," he said as he shook his head. "Once these things show up, they're with you for life."

"What's your psychic thing?"

He smiled at me before answering, "I'm a shield."

My brow puckered in confusion, which caused him to laugh. The humor lit his dark eye so it didn't look so depressed for a moment. "How does that work?"

"Throw a little flame at me, but make sure it's little so I can stamp it out real quick," he instructed.

I looked at him like he was crazy. Hell, we were in a nut house, weren't we? However, he hadn't done anything to seem untrustworthy, so I created a tiny ball of fire in my palm after some concentration. "How do I throw it?"

"Just like a snowball."

I squeezed my eyes shut and prepared to toss the flames at him. "Miss Sable, I can't show you what a shield is if your eyes are shut."

I opened my eyes, and despite my better judgment, I threw the ball at him. He held his palm out toward me. Just before the ball of flames touched his hand, it bounced off an invisible barrier and onto the floor. In one swift motion, he stamped the fire out with his bare foot. My jaw dropped open. I didn't know which was more amazing: the fact that he'd just repelled fire or that he stepped on it and didn't even flinch or wince.

"How—what—how—" I spluttered.

He chuckled. "I used the shield to put the fire out. It never touched my skin."

"Wow." I was stunned. I didn't know what else to say. "Everyone down here can do stuff like that?"

"Not all of it is like that. There's some people that their 'gift' only works in your head. Like Ophelia, she can see the future, but keep that quiet. The good Doctor don't know that about her yet," Fang explained.

Ophelia! His mentioning her name jerked my brain back to seeing her all bruised and sickly. "Fang, is there a way I can go see Ophelia? I need to talk to her! Someone beat her. She's all bruised." My eyes were teary as I finished speaking.

He smiled sadly. "It'll take a little work, but I'll see what I can do."

I had the feeling that Fang couldn't stand to see a girl cry.

We were silent for a long while. Fang fell asleep sitting up. I got off the cot and tried to lay him down gently, but he was too heavy for me to maneuver, so he sort of just flopped over. Thankfully, that didn't wake him up. I started pacing the floor since there was nothing else to do. The sound of waves rolling to the shore drifted in through the window. If I stood on my tip toes, I could just see out of it. As I stared off into the water, I imagined myself swimming away from here. If I could ever plan an escape from here, I'd have to take Fang and Ophelia with me.

The clanging of metal disrupted my reverie. My cell door swung open, and yet another orderly was standing on the other side of the threshold. "Doctor Pantiel wants to see you."

A lump formed in my throat and my mouth went dry. I managed to croak out, "Are we going to his office upstairs?"

The orderly shook his head stiffly. My heart started beating wildly in my chest and my stomach did flips as I was led away down a long and winding corridor. At the end, there was a metal door. That was our destination.

The orderly knocked on the door with three clipped raps. Before I realized what was happening, I was thrust into the room. The lights were blindingly bright compared to the dimly lit surroundings I was now accustomed to. While my eyes were getting used to the change in light, I was being hooked up to monitors and wires were being taped to my chest, head, wrists, and back.

I sat on a steel examination table and looked at the different monitors while the medical staff prepped me for whatever testing Doctor Pantiel had ordered. He wasn't in the room yet. Some of the equipment I recognized from watching medical shows, like the heart and blood pressure monitors. Others were reading data that I didn't know what they were for.

I noticed a man in the corner of the room. He wore an electronic collar around his neck and his muscles looked like he'd abused steroids for quite some time. There was no expression in his eyes. The soul of that man was lost somewhere inside. I concluded that he was like the rest of us trapped down in this prison.

As the medical staff finished their prep work, Doctor Pantiel entered the room. His presence commanded respect and admiration from the staff. He glanced briefly over the chart in his hand—my chart—then he looked at me and smiled with malice.

"Sable Mosley. How are you finding your new accommodations?" he asked with a feigned politeness.

I shrugged. "I've had worse." The heart monitor betrayed my confident air by spiking with my increased heart rate. He knew I was afraid, probably just like the others that were condemned to spend time here.

"How unfortunate," he remarked, disinterested.

"Doctor, the instruments you requested for performing this test are ready," a nurse informed him.

"Thank you," he said. He walked over to a table that sat opposite the exam table and picked a piece of paper up off of it. He held the page in front of my face and instructed, "Set this on fire in the corner furthest away from my fingers. If you try to burn me, there will be swift consequences."

"What makes you think I can, Jude?" I sneered.

Doctor Pantiel snapped his fingers and the man in the corner walked over to me. I could hear electricity crackling through his collar. He bent his head low so he could whisper in my ear. "I'm sorry."

No sooner had the apology left his lips, his fist connected with my stomach. I had a feeling that he was holding back because he choked briefly after he hit me. The air was still gone from my lungs, though. He tried to spare me and was electrocuted for it. This place really was hell.

As I tried to replenish my oxygen, Doctor Pantiel explained, "Kent makes sure that our orders are followed explicitly and swiftly. If you'd like to avoid broken bones, I suggest you light the paper on fire in the manner I instructed."

I blinked the tears out of my eyes to see him smirking. I tried to focus as best I could and concentrated on making a small flame in the correct corner. It didn't take long for the paper to begin burning. Doctor Pantiel dropped it into a bathtub filled with ice water.

"Good," he mused as he turned his attention back to me. He looked at a monitor behind me and jotted notes down into my file. "Next, we'll see how you're affected by the cold."

Before I could object, even though I should've known not to, nurses were stripping my scrubs off of me. When I was naked, an orderly picked me up and set me into the bathtub, careful not to splash the freezing water onto himself. My blood instantly felt like sludge in my veins. I'd always been sensitive to the cold.

"Doctor, she's only been in the water for two minutes and her lips are blue," one of the nurses commented. There was no concern in her voice. She was simply stating a fact.

"Yet the ice is already melted. What's the water temperature?" he asked.

The nurse bent over the tub and checked a thermometer in the water that I hadn't noticed was there. She read, "The water is 117 degrees F. It was 34 degrees F when we put her into the water."

"So her body heat dispersed through the water. What is the subject's temperature?" Doctor Pantiel asked.

After reading a monitor, the nurse replied, "Sixty-nine degrees Fahrenheit, Doctor."

"Since she's been so cooperative, we'll save the next test for tomorrow. You're welcome," he said the last bit to me before he left the room.

An orderly picked me up out of the bathtub and the nurses put my scrubs back on me. Then I was led back to my cell, but I didn't remember getting there. I kept blacking out, so my guess was that I got dragged a lot of the way there. I fully lost consciousness before we got back to my cell.

When I finally came to, I was laying on our cot. Fang and a man I didn't recognize were sitting in front of me on the floor. The man I didn't know sat with his eyes closed. He looked peaceful and pensive at the same time.

"She's waking up," I heard a soft female voice say. I recognized it, but I couldn't place it.

As I regained full consciousness, my body was wracked with tremors. I caught a glimpse of one of my hands. My veins looked like webs of purple and red blanketed over bluish white skin. My teeth started chattering as I shook with cold. Fang swooped me up in his arms and he held me close to him. He felt so warm; it almost burned to be pressed against him.

"Thank you, Roger," the female voice breathed, relief pouring from the statement.

"We've got to look out for each other, Ophelia. If we don't, none of us will survive," Roger replied gravely. His voice was gruff, but kind.

"Ophelia?" I whispered.

"Just relax for now, honey," she said as she knelt next to Fang. She smiled sympathetically at me and took my hand in hers. It felt hot, too. Would I feel any warmer soon?

"What was he testing?" I croaked.

"Your cold tolerance. He'll probably want to know what your heat tolerance is, too. He did that to Holly," Ophelia answered.

"Holly?" I asked.

"She does like you, but with ice. She uses the moisture in the air to make ice," Fang explained.

"Do I want to know?" I moaned.

"Probably not," Ophelia shook her head.

"Did she die?" My voice was so quiet, I barely heard myself ask it. The silence that greeted me answered my question. I cringed in horror.

"Just go on and rest now. We get to keep Ophelia for a while, so don't worry about her going somewhere," Fang soothed. I decided to take his advice and fell back asleep in his arms. At least he didn't feel as blisteringly hot anymore.

V

I couldn't tell how much time had passed when I woke up. Then again, you couldn't really tell how much time passed down here other than the sunrise and sunset. When I rubbed the sleep out of my eyes, I noticed I was lying down on the cot again. My temperature must've returned to normal. I looked around the cell to see where everyone else was. It was too dark. I concentrated on making a small amount of flames in my upturned palm. With the light of the fire, I saw Fang, Ophelia, and Roger sitting in the far corner. They noticed the firelight immediately and came over to me. I extinguished the flames and started to sit up, but I felt a strong hand gently press my shoulder down.

"Don't go rushing into that now, Miss Sable. I reckon they'll throw a tray of food in here soon enough. Then maybe you can get some strength back," Fang said.

"All right," I croaked. My voice was still hoarse.

"How are you feeling?" Ophelia asked.

"Okay I guess," I answered after clearing my throat. It didn't help much.

"Glad to see you pulled through. Doctor Pantiel probably will be, too, but with more sinister sentiments," Roger said darkly.

"What's going on in this place? How is any of this even legal?" I asked.

"We're glorified lab rats," Roger said bluntly.

"How did this happen? Why can I start fires, and why can Ophelia see the future and Fang can make energy shields and you can do…whatever it is you do?" I asked Roger.

"I'm a healer," Roger explained. "And this all started a long time before any of us was born.

"The first documented case of our kind of genetic mutation showed up sometime during the first World War. Supposedly, soldiers that had prolonged exposure to chemical warfare were the ones affected by the genetic mutation. The first one could move the earth. He created all kinds of hell with earthquakes, some of which caused tsunamis. They labeled him 'Tremor.' The plan was for the government to make him into a weapon, but he fought back. Then the goal was to kill him, study his corpse, and make an army they could control. Tremor ran.

"I guess after he was well hidden, he settled down and reproduced because there's quite a few of us now. Not enough to be classified as our own race or anything, but enough to make the governments of the world afraid of us. I'd imagine that there are places like this all over the globe, keeping us captive. This is the biggest one in the US. There's another one in Alaska and one in Texas, too. Amongst ourselves, we refer to each other as being 'gifted.' The government has labeled us 'The Diseased.'"

"So when people talk about diseased people, they're talking about…our kind?"

"No," Roger replied. "We're kept secret, like Area 51 and shit like that. The general public doesn't know we exist. If there's one of us who tries to make themselves known, they're assassinated."

"If all this stuff is secret, how do you know so much about it?" I asked skeptically.

"Roger is kind of like a double agent. He acts as one of the orderlies here. He used to be in the CIA, but he opted for early retirement," Ophelia said softly. When she mentioned his retiring, something in Roger's mood seemed to shift to a dark place, so I didn't press the issue.

"But why do we all have different abilities? If it's the same mutation, then why not the same ability?"

"The research doesn't explain that," Roger answered. "The scientists have chalked it up to members of the same family excelling in different areas. Of three siblings, one may have a mind for words, one for numbers, and one for music. The abilities seem to show up at random,"

Fang chuckled. "You ask a whole lot of questions, Miss Sable."

I suddenly felt embarrassed by my inquisition. I tried to sit up again, and this time Fang allowed it. My vision got a little fuzzy around the edges and the room spun a little, but otherwise, I was okay. Ophelia sat next to me and put her arm around my shoulders.

"We need to get out of here," I sighed.

"We need a plan, first," Ophelia pointed out.

"Speaking of getting out of here, I need to take Ophelia back to her cell. They'll be coming around with food rations in a bit. I'll try to get her back in here soon," Roger promised as he took Ophelia's hand in his. With a heavy sigh, she left our cell with Roger. The door clanged shut behind them.

"I didn't even get to thank him for healing me," I mumbled as I scrubbed a hand down my face.

"He knows you're grateful," Fang reassured me.

I still felt tired, but I couldn't fall back asleep. The thought of my next testing session kept creeping into my mind. Then I remembered about Holly. Who was she? What was her story? Did I really want to know?

A few minutes passed by and a tray of slop was shoved under our door. Fang ate a small portion of it and insisted I eat the rest. The texture of the moldy looking substance was like cottage cheese, but the flavor was far from it. Whatever this stuff was, it was definitely rotted. I tried my best not to gag too much while I forced it down.

Desperate to think about anything other than what it was I just consumed, I asked Fang, "What happened to Holly?"

A shadow crossed over his face as he settled his fist under his chin in thought. "Holly was about the same age as you, I reckon. She controlled the vapor in the air around her, could freeze it. She was staying in a cell with a, uh, buddy of mine, Hunter. He sort of had a crush on her. It hurt him real bad when she'd go for testing. She'd come back exhausted, and often showing marks where the orderlies beat her." Fang sighed. "Then they did that test where they wanted to know how cold she could make the water around her if it was boiling,"

"And they...boiled her to death?" I asked. The horror I felt inside was evident in my tone.

"That's the story. No one's seen her since."

"What about Hunter? What could he do?" I whispered.

"Hunter could make himself invisible. We don't know if he ran off or if he was killed, too," Fang admitted.

I slumped back down on the mattress. What the hell was wrong with these people? The pain in Fang's voice when he spoke of Hunter made my heart break. I decided it would be better not to press him for more details about people of his past for now. "Fang, get some sleep, okay?"

He chuckled. "Never you mind about my sleeping, Miss Sable." He sat up against the wall, next to end of the cot where my head was and closed his eyes. Before too long, he was snoring softly.

I tried to wrack my brain for some way to escape from this place. There was nothing, though, that I could think of to make it happen. I looked longingly at the window. It was too high up to reach and definitely too small for anything bigger than a cat to squeeze through. Sighing wearily, I decided to get some sleep myself.

I regretted falling asleep later. I dreamed that I was in Holly's place, being boiled alive like I was the protein in a stew for cannibals. The nurses around me just stared and jotted things down on charts while my skin became red hot and I lost the ability to breathe. The blood in my veins bubbled as my internal temperature climbed. Eventually, cardiac arrest took hold, and the lines on all the monitors I was hooked up to went flat. They all made a discordant beeping noise that seemed to drag out for forever.

I woke up panting, my body covered in a sheen of sweat. My already thick, chocolate brown hair was made thicker with snarls and it stuck to the back of my neck and my face. I rolled over as quickly as I could and retched on the floor. Not surprisingly, the rotted food tasted worse when mixed with bile. I desperately wanted a toothbrush and toothpaste.

I thought longingly of being at home in my own bed, instead of being on this cot. I missed my feather pillows and my comforter that had Vincent Van Gough's Starry Night painting printed on it. It was amazing, the things you always took for granted that you wanted desperately to cling to when your whole world was turned upside down. I longed for normalcy, but that ship had sailed long ago.

Fang was still sleeping next to the cot. I was glad I didn't wake him up. He'd done quite enough for me the past couple of days. The poor guy deserved some rest. I'd have to find a way to repay him for that someday. *If you ever get out of here alive*, I thought miserably. If I kept thinking that way, though, I really never would get out. My mother always taught me that I could accomplish anything, if I was willing to put in the effort to make it happen.

I lay back down on the cot and stared up at the ceiling. It was dirty and rough stone, just like the other walls. I willed a small flame to appear in my palm. When it did, I could see that the rock glittered in a way. It was probably full of crushed seashells, encased in the solid earth over the years, like fossils. When I extinguished the flame, I noticed the light filtering through the window was a light colored blue, the sign that dawn was approaching.

Somehow, I managed to drift back to sleep, because I was startled awake when Fang shook my arm gently. I swatted at his hand then realized it was him. Sheepishly, I said, "I'm sorry."

"Sorry for waking you, Miss Sable, but Roger said he was coming for you early this morning. I think he's taking you to Ophelia's cell," Fang smiled.

"Aren't you going to come?" I asked as I sat up and stretched.

"Nah, it's too dangerous to move more than one prisoner at a time if there's not some big spectacle going on," he answered.

As if Fang's mention of his name summoned him, the cell door swung open, Roger standing on the other side. His expression was hard, but the look in his eyes was uneasy. I had a feeling I wasn't going to see Ophelia.

"Mosley, get out here!" Roger barked. I tripped over my feet as I stood up and lumbered toward him. When I approached the cell door, he took me roughly by the arm and started dragging me down the corridor after him.

"We're going to see Doctor Pantiel, aren't we?" I whispered. His only response was a curt nod of his head.

When we got to the testing room, Roger stopped in front of the door. He put a key in the handle. While he turned the knob, he mouthed to me that he was sorry. I knew he was playing his role as a double agent, but I couldn't help but feeling a little betrayed.

Once the door was closed—Roger didn't stay—I was made to strip out of my scrubs. I'd wondered the night before if being naked in front of people would get easier the more times I had to do it. Right now, it was just as uncomfortable as the day before. Goose bumps broke out across my skin in the chilly room. Nurses scrambled to get me hooked up to all the monitors before Doctor Pantiel arrived.

While I was being prepped, I wondered what was supposed to be the test for today. An image of my dream floated across my vision. A shudder ran down my spine and I swallowed back the bile rising in my throat. I wished I could mentally steel myself to be prepared for whatever was coming, but I wasn't so brave. A tear ran down my cheek as Doctor Pantiel entered the room.

"Sable, why on earth are you crying?" he asked as he closed the door behind him and flipped through my chart. His tone was one of feigned concern. My hand twitched with the urge to punch him.

"My eyes were watering. I'm allergic to assholes, Jude," I replied stonily. My stomach lurched every time something like that came out of my mouth around him. He had all the control in this situation, but I still had to be mouthy. He might've just chalked it up to teenage angst since the only reaction he gave was a tick in the muscle of his jaw. The truth was, I'd been that way my whole life and been reprimanded for it just as long.

"Do you have the syringes prepared?" Doctor Pantiel asked the nurse who was sitting in front of me.

"Yes, Doctor," she replied. She waved her hand toward a tray of medical instruments as she took my blood pressure and pulse. I looked over to the tray. Aside from scalpels and other instruments you'd see on any medical drama on TV, there were five syringes filled with what looked like water.

"What's with the injections?" I asked no one in particular. My voice shook when I spoke.

"We're going to see how your blood responds to them," Doctor Pantiel said simply.

"You're going to inject me with acid?" I demanded incredulously.

"No, that would eat right through your system. The syringes," he said, with a sadistic smirk on his face, "are full of liquid nitrogen."

"What in God's name is the purpose of that?" I yelled.

"Is the blood in your veins the source of your fire power? If it is, when we inject you, your blood shouldn't freeze. True, it might turn to sludge, but it won't become solid," he explained. He spoke as calmly as if I asked him what the weather report was today.

All the air left my lungs and my eyes bulged in panic. I wished Fang was here to shield me from these horrible people. Suddenly, I realized that I was sobbing. And I was going to die. I silently began praying. I wondered if everyone prayed for redemption when they knew they were dying.

When the nurse lifted the first syringe off of the instrument tray, I began hyperventilating. My body was practically vibrating with fear. Just as the needle pierced my skin, the overhead lights began to flicker. I noticed that all the monitors were flashing, too. The nurse turned her attention to the shorting electricity. Some of the other nurses mumbled about the facility being old and needing repair, while others discussed the possibility of an impending storm. When it stabilized, she positioned her thumb on the plunger.

This is it, I thought. I'm going to die right now.

Then everything went black.

VI

At first, everything was still, and I assumed I was dead. Then the sounds of people screaming permeated the atmosphere and I thought I was in Hell.

"Get the lights back on! Secure the Diseased!" Doctor Pantiel shrieked. So I wasn't in Hell, after all. I heard the nurse that was holding the syringe scurry away to do the Doctor's bidding. I ripped the syringe out of my arm, hissing in a breath at the sting, and threw it away from me. The other nurses and orderlies fled the room, too, taking the Doctor with them.

A loud pop sounded, and the door handle banged against the wall. I still couldn't see anything in the blackness. Then a crackling figure appeared in the doorway. It looked like the shape of a human being. Blue and white currents of electricity popped off of the figure. It seemed like it was coursing through the person like blood.

Quick as lightning, a shockwave was thrown into the room blindly and hit one of the monitors I was hooked up to. Thankfully, all I got from it was a shock, but it still hurt. I yelped, more out of surprise than pain.

"Just like you cowards, talking all high when we're under your thumb, but when we're unbridled, you're terrified," the glowing figure snarled. It sounded like a young man speaking, a rich sort of vibrato in his tone that was familiar somehow.

"Who are you?" My voice trembled when I spoke.

"Who's asking?" the man asked.

"Me." It sounded sort of obstinate, but that wasn't how I intended it to be.

"And who the hell is 'me'?" the man demanded.

My fist turned into a ball of flames. I held it near my face, being careful not to set my hair alight, and answered, "Sable Mosley."

"Are you producing that flame, Sable Mosley?" Since he was glowing with electricity, I didn't see the harm in admitting so. I nodded in response.

Suddenly, the figure was gone. I could see the shadow of the outline of his body moving toward me. With too quick movements, he seized me by the wrist. The flames on my hand extinguished, but not before setting the paper on the exam table beneath me alight. He cursed under his breath and jerked me off the table.

With sudden dismay, I realized that I was still nude. "I have to get my clothes!" I said in a panicked voice.

"You what?" the man asked incredulously.

I made flames appear in my upturned palm and frantically searched for my scrubs. Thank God they were still sitting near the door, just where I'd left them.

"Come on, we have to go," he shouted impatiently. I could hear the heavy pounding of running footsteps somewhere in the distance, and they were increasing in volume. They were coming back to get me. As hastily as I could, I pulled the scrubs on. The man grabbed my wrist once more and pulled me toward the door.

"Where are we going?" I implored as we began running away from the testing room, which was, unfortunately, in the path of the oncoming orderlies.

"Out," he said flatly as he pulled me along behind him.

"We have to get my friends," I blurted out suddenly. There was no way I was going to leave Fang and Ophelia behind. I didn't know if Roger would come, but I didn't have time to look for him. I knew where Fang was, and he knew where Ophelia was.

"We don't have time for this," the man warned.

"I can't go without them," I whimpered.

"What use are they to me?"

"One can see the future and one makes kinetic shields." Hopefully, that was enough to persuade him.

"Fine. Where are they?" he growled. I directed him to my cell, him pulling me the whole way.

"What's your name anyway?" I asked with a rasping breath. All the adrenaline and the fear and the running were really wearing me out.

"Brandon Harper," he said as we stopped in front of my cell door. He yanked it open with a force. Just behind the door, Fang's silhouette stood in what looked like a battle stance, like he was ready to fight.

"Get your hands off the girl," Fang said. Although the words were quiet, they were filled with authority.

"Fang, this is Brandon. He's breaking us out of here. We have to find Ophelia!" I explained quickly.

Fang considered Brandon for a moment and then hurried back in the direction we came, motioning for us to follow him. Brandon took off like a shot, dragging me behind him.

About ten or twelve doors down—we were running too fast for me to accurately count—Fang stopped short in front of a cell door and threw it open. "Ophelia, we're bustin' out of here. Hurry!"

Ophelia trotted out to meet us, her face flooding with relief when she saw me and then skepticism as she studied Brandon. As we ran back the way we'd just come, she asked, "Where is Chloe?"

"Outside with the boat," Brandon answered before Fang or I could ask who Chloe was.

I could hear thudding sounds above us. The door to the stairway banged open, and the thudding steps grew louder. The orderlies were coming back to secure the prisoners in the basement. Brandon cursed under his breath.

"We're going to have to fight our way out," he hissed.

"Wait, what? I can't fight anyone!" I protested. Physically, I wasn't very strong, certainly not enough to contend with the orderlies, who all seemed to be pretty muscular.

"I would say fight fire with fire, but they don't have any. So fight orderlies with fire," Brandon spat.

Fang looked geared up for a fight. Without using his kinetic shields, I suspected he'd be able to take out a few people. Combine that with his pent up aggression from being locked up for so long, he was probably lethal. It was such a contrast from the seemingly gentle giant he'd been toward me. Ophelia wasn't in any shape to fight, either.

"Wait!" Ophelia said. "We can hide in one of these cells. There's one close to the foot of the stairs that's been abandoned for quite some time. We'll wait for them to pass by and make a quiet escape. We don't want to set off any more alarms."

Brandon looked like he was weighing his options but decided to follow Ophelia's lead. The cell she was talking about was only a few doors ahead. Fang opened it and ushered the rest of us inside before closing it. I held my breath as I watched the orderlies thunder past us, the one in front yelling instructions to all the ones who followed him.

When the last sounds of footsteps died away, we slipped out of the cell and bounded up the stairs as quietly as we could manage. Before we turned any corners, Brandon always checked skillfully for coming threats. When he was satisfied the coast was clear, we'd hurry onward. After what seemed like an hour, we finally reached the outdoors.

The sun of high noon stung my eyes, but I couldn't have been happier to have the warmth streaming down on my skin. I had barely started enjoying the smell of the air outdoors and the feeling of being freed before we started running again. Brandon kept looking over his shoulder to make sure we were keeping pace. Fang kept stride right along with him, Ophelia falling a short distance behind. I brought up the rear and had unpleasant flashbacks of being in gym class. As the shore drew nearer, a white speedboat with teal pinstripes on its side was visible. When we got closer, I could see its name printed in purple: *Sparky*. I thought that name was odd for a boat and more appropriate for a dog.

"Chloe, start the engine!" Brandon called as we approached. The engine roared to life, drowning out the sounds of our footsteps. Brandon jumped into the boat first, then Fang. Fang helped Ophelia over, then me. Brandon took the wheel of the boat and started backing it away from the shore.

"What the hell is this, Brandon?" Chloe snapped. "You weren't supposed to bring anyone back with you!" She was about my height, just a little shorter. Her cheeks burned pink, masked slightly by the splash of freckles across her nose and cheekbones. She glared at Brandon, her hands clasped tightly on her hips in aggravation.

"Change of plans," Brandon shrugged.

"Who's Chloe?" I whispered to Ophelia as the boat sped off into the ocean.

"That's Brandon's sister."

The family resemblance must've been really subtle because they looked very different from each other. Chloe was short with straight coarse red hair that looked like a flame on the ocean, while Brandon was tall with black hair, with fine strands that curled. His skin looked tan while his sister's was pale white. Her eyes were the color of liquid amber, while his were an icy shade of blue, like the electricity that coursed through him just before it burned white. There were some similarities, however. They both had sharp angular facial features, both with slender builds with lean musculature; Brandon's a bit bulkier than Chloe's.

That's when it finally hit me. How did I not make the connection before? Brandon was the incredibly good looking orderly! I gaped at him, taking in his features. Instead of navy blue scrubs, he'd donned baggy jeans and a V-neck, white T-shirt. This look suited him much better. My stomach fluttered wildly as I studied his lean musculature, his slender throat, his lips pressed into a hard line—

"Brandon? I thought your name was Nathaniel," I accused.

"Nathaniel is my middle name, and is also my father's name." He smiled at the admission before returning his attention to the open sea. His smile melted my insides.

I had to get my mind on something else. I didn't want him to see me staring at him. Instead, I decided to take advantage of the sunlight to really see my new friends. They looked just shy of being emaciated, Ophelia more so than Fang. Fang's skin looked like it was a rich brown color, now muted by ashy gray. His good eye was as dark as black coffee, which sank into his brow line a little. You could tell he'd been pretty muscled at one point, but being imprisoned had eaten them away some. Black tribal tattoos covered both his arms. The thick scars down the side of his face were a few shades lighter than the rest of his skin.

Ophelia's dark blonde hair dusted the ends of her shoulder blades. Her features were reminiscent of a porcelain doll. Her violet eyes were round and bright, her fingers long and slender. I imagined that when she looked like herself, her cheeks were a little fuller, as were her hips. She was about a half a head taller than me. Her pale skin looked chalky in the sunlight.

"Where are we going?" I asked no one in particular.

"To our battleship," Chloe said without humor. If looks could kill, I think Brandon might be dead. She never did stop glowering at him.

I found myself staring at him, too. His eyes were fierce, and the set of his jaw was tight. He looked like a predator. Something in me said I wouldn't mind being his prey. There was an air of confidence about him, strong and proud with the knowledge that he was attractive. I was suddenly aware at how horrendous I looked at the moment and cringed.

Ophelia cleared her throat, breaking me out of my reverie. I looked at her and she smiled softly. "There's a ship that sits in international waters. They disguise it as a fishing ship, so no one really bothers them. What they really do is train people like us to be weapons, but unlike the governments of the world, they aren't exploiting us. It's basically teaching us self-defense."

"Who are 'they'?" I asked.

"The one who spearheads it is named Drake Shaw. He can look inside your soul with a single touch. He knows what your true intentions are, and if they're dark, he sends you back to where you came from," Ophelia explained.

"How do you know all this?" I wondered aloud.

"I've already been sent back once," she replied a little ruefully.

"Do you think he'll send you back to Doctor Pantiel?" I gasped.

She shrugged. "People change. And when I was sent away before, I was living on the streets on my own."

I wanted to ask her more about it, but her tone and the look on her face suggested that she was done talking. I scrubbed my hand down my face and let my thumb linger over my lip piercings: two tiny diamond studs close together on the left side of my bottom lip. The piercer at the tattoo shop called it a spider bite. I bit my lip when I was nervous so I thought it might help to break me of the habit. Turns out I just started biting my lip on the other side.

There wasn't much chatter the rest of the way to the ship. Fang and Ophelia had a few short whispered conversations and Brandon and Chloe got into a few squabbles. I caught myself glancing at Brandon a little too often. Like the rest of us, he looked a little disheveled, but it looked good on him. The spray off the ocean caused his shirt to cling to his body, tracing the hard lines of his body. As I studied him, he gave me a side-long glance. Quickly, I wrenched my gaze to my feet, a blush blossoming in my cheeks.

The sun hung low in the sky when *Sparky* slowed down and was engulfed in a long dark shadow. We were approaching the ship, named *Kandis Amelia.* As we pulled up to a rusted looking ladder on the side of the ship, I wondered why there were so many ships named after a woman. Were they really named after women the ship owners were close with, or were they arbitrary names?

Chloe turned off the motor and dropped the anchor.

"Go tell Shaw we're back," Brandon told her.

"I'm not taking responsibility for the stragglers." Acid dripped from her words.

Brandon shrugged, but his nonchalance was betrayed by the steely look in his eyes.

Chloe climbed the ladder with the swiftness and grace of a cat. It rattled and shook beneath her, but it held fast. After she was out of our view, Brandon gave a wry smile to Ophelia and I. "Ladies first."

We looked at one another and, with an air of determination, Ophelia ascended the ladder. When she was about halfway up, Brandon gave me a look of impatience. I looked at Fang while I chewed on my lip. He gave me an encouraging nod, so I took in a shaky breath and started to climb. Despite the rust that crumbled beneath my hands, the ladder seemed pretty sturdy. As I finally made it to the top, I saw Ophelia staring off into the distance. She was alone on deck. I stopped just behind her, not wanting to disturb her reverie. Fang and Brandon appeared on deck a short time later.

My gaze focused on the hollow of Brandon's throat instead of his eyes. "What now?"

"Now Brandon tells me why he decided to bring you here," a deep voice said from behind me.

Brandon crossed his arms over his chest. "Can't we talk about this in your office?"

I turned to look at the man Brandon spoke to. His hair was a balanced mix of salt and pepper that was cropped close to his head and flat on the top. He looked like a seaman, his skin weathered and deeply tanned. His dark eyes were deep set and didn't seem to miss a single detail. Thick muscles covered his arms, neck, chest, and core. He wore a black T-shirt, black denim-cotton blend pants, and black rubber boots.

"Very well," he allowed. "Ophelia, it's nice to see you found your way back to us. Perhaps you'll fare better now than you did at our last meeting."

"I intend to, Shaw," Ophelia replied, quiet but determined.

VII

Shaw's office was below deck, and the four of us followed as he led the way down a few corridors and two staircases. His office looked like someone cut it out of a corner office space in a corporate building and built it into the ship. There were even large circular windows which gave a view of the ocean and the various forms of sea life that happened by. A broad charting desk sat near the wall opposite the windows with two lawn chairs in front of it.

"Ladies, go ahead and have a seat." Shaw pointed to the lawn chairs. Ophelia and I gingerly sat. Fang stood between us behind the chairs. Brandon stood to the left of the desk, smoothing the wrinkles out of his shirt. Shaw took a swig of something out of a chipped white porcelain coffee mug as he sat in the chair behind the desk. "Brandon, why did you bring them?"

"I can't help myself around damsels in distress," Brandon said, his tone sardonic.

"Please, Mr. Shaw, I begged him to take me with him. Then I insisted he rescue my friends, too. I just couldn't leave them behind in that prison." The last words left me feeling like I swallowed acid.

Shaw scrubbed his chin with his thumb and index finger thoughtfully. "Who are you? Your fire intrigues me."

"My name is Sable Mosley. How did you know I used fire?"

"I didn't, but that's interesting as well. Did you know that about her, Brandon?"

Brandon nodded. "That's how she convinced me to bring her along."

Shaw chuckled. "She threatened to burn you?"

"No! I showed him I could control fire so he wouldn't electrocute me!" I protested.

"Well, we wouldn't have wanted that," Shaw muttered. "So I know what Ophelia can do. What about you, sir?"

"I make kinetic shields. My name is Fang."

"I see. You came from that asylum, yes? I think you all deserved a good night's sleep. We'll assess your skills in the morning. Brandon, show our guests to the spare rooms and have Chloe get them a decent meal." With that, Shaw left us alone in his office. The thudding of his footsteps on the metal floors grew softer at a rapid pace.

Brandon sighed and scrubbed the back of his head with his palm. Without a word, he moved to the office door and waited for us to follow. When he was satisfied we were trailing behind him, he led us through another maze of corridors that led back up toward the deck of the ship. All the hallways looked the same. They were made of steel and weren't painted, so they had an industrial feel. A door was stuck in the walls here and there, interrupting the smooth metal sheets. Finally, we were led down a corridor with many doors. We stopped at a door about halfway down the corridor.

"This will be his room." Brandon indicated the door to his left and nodded to Fang. "The door across from it will be the ladies' room."

After his instructions were dispensed, he started back down the corridor. When we couldn't see him anymore, Fang smiled at Ophelia and me. "Go on and get some sleep now. Soon enough they'll come by with hot meals and in the morning, we'll show Mr. Shaw what we're capable of."

"All right." I wasn't so sure this is how the situation would be. After all, we'd just come from a place that was supposed to help people and look how that turned out.

Fang waited for us to go into our room before he went into his. He really was a southern gentleman.

When Ophelia opened the door to our room, it looked sort of like a hotel. There were full sized beds with plush looking mattresses on them. The blue and green quilts looked like seawater and were neatly turned down over the pillows. Crisp white sheets lay beneath. A small wooden table with a clear glass lamp filled with seashells sat in between the beds. The floor and the walls were the same sheeted steel. A little closet was on the wall adjacent to the door on the right.

A small cry of joy escaped me when I noticed the small bathroom. As much as I needed some quality sleep, I needed a proper shower even worse. Ophelia collapsed on her bed, so I took advantage of the empty shower. Since I didn't have any clothes to change in to, I rummaged through the closet to see if there was anything in it. On the shelf were extra blankets and linens. Hanging on the metal bar were thin looking bathrobes, one for each of us. There weren't any clothes, however. I decided the bathrobe was good enough for now.

I closed the bathroom door quietly behind me. Ophelia was already snoring softly. I turned the hot water on and let it steam up the room. On the sink counter were little scented soaps, travel sized bottles of shampoo and conditioner, a hair-brush, toothbrushes, and toothpaste. After the room was filled with steam, I slipped out of my dirty yellow scrubs and hopped into the tub.

The water beat down on my head and my back. I stood there for a few minutes just letting it pour over me. I kept my eyes closed so I wouldn't see all the dirt running off me. Carefully, I massaged the floral smelling shampoo into my hair. I tried to comb out the snarls with my fingers, but it did little good.

After I rinsed it through and washed it once more for good measure, I scrubbed every inch of my skin clean. Then I decided I should wash my scrubs. I grabbed them off the floor and used one of the small scented soaps to clean the fabric. After wringing out the excess water, I hung them over the shower rod to dry.

I took a towel off of the towel bar that hung over top of the toilet and dried myself off. I wrapped my hair in the towel, making a turban out of it. When I slipped on my robe, I dared to look at myself in the mirror. My face looked gaunt and ashen. The stars tattooed around the right side of my right eye looked too black.

My emerald green eyes were dull looking. There were dark bruises under them from lack of sleep and too much stress. The hollows of my cheeks looked more pronounced than I remembered them. In an attempt to distract myself from the disturbing image in the mirror, I freed my hair from the towel and set to work on untangling it with the brush. After a lot of swearing and a few tears later, my chocolate curls were tamed, although stringy looking since they were still damp.

The bedroom seemed cold after being enveloped in the hot steam. Normally, I wouldn't have gone to bed with my hair wet, but I was too exhausted to care. I snuggled beneath the thick comforter and relished in the soft mattress. Sleep came easily soon after.

A soft knock on the metal door wrenched me awake. I blinked my eyes a few times, expecting to be back in the dim cell in the Crazy Cannon Place's basement.

When I was sure I wasn't still asleep and my surroundings were truly real, I padded to the door and opened it just a crack. A boy who looked about my age stood on the other side. His soft brown eyes twinkled in the harsh light of the fluorescents in the corridors.

"I brought you something to eat. I came by last night with some dinner, but you both were sleeping so soundly, I thought it would be a shame to wake you." His lips parted into a smile with rows of perfectly straight white teeth. It was as kind as his voice and his eyes. I cracked the door open enough for me to slip into the hallway without waking up Ophelia with the lights.

"It's morning?" My voice sounded groggy, the kind of groggy that well rested people had.

"Yes. And I brought you breakfast. Might I ask your name?"

"It's Sable Mosley. What's yours?"

"Kelly Anderson. I'll be back in a bit to escort you to the training room. Shaw wants to see what you can do." He ran a hand through his toffee colored hair. I noticed his musculature wasn't as pronounced as Brandon's.

His style was more laid back, like someone on vacation in Florida. He wore a red ribbed tank top and khaki Bermuda shorts with tan leather sandals. Rectangle white framed glasses sat on the bridge of his slightly crooked nose. He held a tray in his hands with two covered dishes and two glasses of milk.

"Thanks." I took the tray from him and smiled. When I was back in our room, Kelly pulled the door closed behind me.

It took my eyes a minute to adjust to the dim light of the table lamp. I set the tray on the table and then I put a hand on Ophelia's shoulder, shaking her lightly. She yawned and rubbed her eyes, trying to wipe away the sleep.

"What's up?" she said through another yawn.

"Breakfast."

She stretched and sat up, glancing at the tray on the table. "What is it?"

"I haven't looked yet." I pulled the cover off of one of the platters and squealed with joy when I saw what was underneath. A fluffy lobster and spinach omelet drizzled with hollandaise sauce sat in the center of the plate. The same type of omelet was on the other plate, too. "We're getting real food?"

"This place is nothing like where we just came from." Ophelia popped a bite of omelet into her mouth. Her eyes closed as she savored the taste of it. I tried my hardest not to inhale mine, but after a week without really eating, it was a difficult task. The lobster was sweet and delicate, the spinach giving off an herb like flavor, and the eggs fluffy and light. The sauce was smooth and rich. I was glad we were given milk to drink with it.

Ophelia ate her breakfast faster than me. While I finished mine, she took a shower. I put my cleaned scrubs back on after I was done eating. I desperately wished for different clothes. Something a little more flattering on my thin frame.

Just as Ophelia emerged from the bathroom, a knock sounded on the door. When I opened it, Kelly stood on the other side. "Hey there. Did you enjoy your breakfast?"

I nodded and smiled. "So, are you here to bring us to Shaw?"

"Yes. Are you ready?"

"As ready as I can be, I guess." I looked over my shoulder to Ophelia, who was coming to the door.

Kelly led us down yet another maze of corridors. I could feel the gentle sway of the ship bobbing with the undercurrents in the water. The farther we walked, the tighter the knot in my stomach became. I wondered how Shaw meant to test what we were able to do.

"Kelly, where is Fang?" I asked.

"Chloe was to show him to the training room before I brought you ladies in. He should be waiting for you when we arrive."

Hopefully Fang would be able to stick around where Ophelia and I were. He'd become like a big brother to me when we were in the asylum together. It seemed like he and Ophelia were close, too. It was almost like we were becoming a family, albeit a strange one.

When we got to the training room, Kelly opened the door and waited for us to enter before he came in. I sighed a relieved breath I wasn't aware I was holding onto when I saw Fang. A sheen of sweat coated him, but he looked more alive than I'd ever seen him. The rest did him good, just like Ophelia and me. I ran over to him and threw my arms around his waist.

"Well, hello to you, too, Miss Sable." He smiled as he pulled me back from him and studied my face. Then he looked at Ophelia with his warm smile on his lips.

"Good to see you, Fang." She waved at him and smiled. The happiness didn't reach her eyes, though. There was a sense of steel in them that I couldn't quite place.

Fang and I walked over to Ophelia. He spoke to her in a low voice. "You'll make it through this time, Phea."

So that was the reason for her distance. I couldn't blame her. I wouldn't want to be sent back to the Crazy Cannon Place. Doctor Pantiel would undoubtedly be extremely angry we broke out. There's nothing to say that he wouldn't kill us all if we went back. I cringed and pushed the thought to the back of my mind. I had to be focused now. Distractions like that were counterproductive.

Shaw was standing at the opposite end of the room with Brandon and Chloe. They were watching Fang, Ophelia, and me with apparent curiosity.

Kelly stood with his arms crossed over his chest in front of the door. When he saw me looking at him, he cast his eyes downward quickly and a faint blush colored his cheeks. I could feel my own start to burn a little.

"Ophelia," Shaw said, moving toward us as he spoke, "will we be keeping you this time?"

"Yes." Her tone was steely and determined.

"Is that your prediction or is it what you most hope for?"

"Both." She said this with some vulnerability. I couldn't imagine being rejected by the same person twice. I could barely stay around for the first rejection to be completed. Then Shaw turned his attention to me.

"See that plant in the corner over there? I want you to set it on fire."

"Excuse me?" My voice caught in my throat.

He crossed his arms over his chest, challenging me. "You said you start fires, so start one."

I took a deep breath and concentrated on the plant. The foliage blurred in my vision. I made myself concentrate on a single leaf.

After a few tense moments, a small flame danced on the tip of the leaf and quickly extinguished itself.

Shaw barked an unkind laugh. "That's all you can do? All you're good for is lighting cigarettes and candles! Brandon, this is what you bring to me for training? I didn't realize you were one for charity cases. I thought I made it clear that I didn't do charity. Perhaps you can lend her an empathetic ear when I toss you both out—"

I couldn't listen to him insult me or Brandon anymore, although I wasn't sure why I felt such indignation on his behalf.

Without my entirely meaning it to, the plant burst into flames and burned brightly. At least it startled Shaw enough to get him to shut up.

As I looked around the room at everyone's faces, a degree of shock—ranging from mild, Fang, to astonished, Kelly—lit everyone's features. The sound of water splashing interrupted my observation.

Chloe held an orb of water suspended in the air and threw it down over the burning plant. The flames were doused and a smoking stem was all that was left of the plant.

"Well, well, it seems I was mistaken, then." Shaw looked me over, his expression thoughtful. Then he held his hand out to me. "Your hand, if you please."

I looked at Fang and Ophelia, who both nodded. I tentatively placed my hand in his and chewed on my lip. Shaw's eyes went vacant, like they were staring at something very far away.

When he snapped back to the present, he let go of my hand and took Ophelia's. After a similar exchange, he let go of Ophelia's hand and smiled.

He turned towards Brandon and Chloe before he spoke again. "It seems our guests will be permanent residents here now. I'm delighted this is the case. I would hate to think you were losing your touch, Brandon. And Chloe...well, you wouldn't have stuck around long without your big brother here to keep a watch over you, now would you?

"Kelly, take them shopping. No one in my arsenal will appear as if they crawled out of the sewers." With that, Shaw

moved past Kelly and out the door, leaving us all staring behind him.

VIII

I never considered myself a fan of shopping, but I found that I seriously enjoyed doing it on this particular trip. When we were back on the ship and I looked at myself in the mirror, it was the first time in a long time I felt like myself. I wore a black long-sleeved, fishnet shirt over an eggplant-colored tube top and a simple black skirt that was slit up to my thigh on the left side.

Black boots with a slight platform on them and five sets of buckles that rose to just below my knee were slipped over lime green fishnet stockings. A silver sparkling star pendant hung from a corded silver chain around my neck.

Ophelia came up behind me and was primping a little herself. She'd bleached her dirty blonde locks so they were almost white and put pink and teal streaks in it. The cut reminded me of Cyndi Lauper's hair on the cover of her *She's So Unusual* album.

A slouchy gray sweater was thrown on over her black tank top, and teal leggings coordinated with her multi-colored neon Chuck Taylor high tops. Her violet eyes shone with nostalgia as she looked at her reflection.

A soft knock sounded at the door, so I went to answer it. I expected it to be either Fang or Kelly, so I was surprised when Brandon was the one on the other side of the door. He took a few moments to let his eyes drag up and down my body.

It made my nerves crackle and my skin feel tight over my muscles. His voice caught a little when he spoke. "Shaw wants me to bring the three of you to training."

"He wants us to train to work together?"

"Something like that."

"Hold on a second." I left him standing in the doorway and grabbed Ophelia. While I explained that Shaw wanted us to train, Brandon got Fang out of his room. We all met in the hallway, and Brandon led us down to the corridor. The room he took us to was across the hall from the one we'd been in the day before.

When Brandon opened the door, I immediately noticed all the work out equipment. It was like a miniature gym. Even though I wasn't the gym type, I had to admit it was impressive to find on a ship in the middle of the Atlantic. Upon further inspection, I noticed weapons lining the walls ranging from knives to throwing stars, pistols, broadswords, and everything else in between. Fang let out a low whistle as we all stepped through the doorway. Shaw, Kelly, and Chloe were waiting for us. I wondered if there wasn't a room I'd be led to that didn't have someone waiting for me in it.

Once we were all inside, Shaw explained to us that he wanted us to be able to use weapons other than our natural gifts, just in case. In case of what, I couldn't guess. Kelly was assigned to Fang, Chloe to Ophelia, and Brandon to me. Shaw wanted to see what our current skill level in fighting was, so he directed us to wrestling mats on the floor in one corner of the room.

Fang and Kelly were the first to spar with each other. Kelly was a pretty good fighter with quick reflexes, but Fang held his own very well. It wasn't long before Kelly was on the defensive, Fang jabbing and kicking like a seasoned mixed martial artist would. Shaw was satisfied rather quickly that Fang wouldn't require much training.

Ophelia and Chloe were up next. Ophelia didn't fare as well as Fang. She was pinned down one round kick and a left hook later. A smug look of satisfaction crossed Chloe's face as she rose from her crouching position. She looked over at Brandon and her smirk fell away. From the corner of my eye, I could tell his attention was on me and not on Chloe or Shaw, who was praising her on her fighting tactics. A blush spread across my cheeks.

Goosebumps littered my skin and I bit my lip when Brandon and I took our places on the mats. My fate would be sealed faster than Ophelia's. I'd never even been in a fight at school or anything, let alone trained for combat. Brandon lunged for me, wrapping his arms around my waist, and tackling me to the floor.

In a show of stereotypical female frailty, I put my arms up in defense just before he made contact with me and shrieked. We were sprawled on the floor, my arms pinned between our bodies, his hands locked together behind my back. Our faces were less than an inch apart, his eyes boring into mine. If I had the option to move, his ice blue eyes would have kept me pinned ungracefully beneath him.

"You're a crap fighter." His voice rasped, his breath hot on my skin.

I was too stunned to make any sort of reply.

"Kelly, you'll be working with Ophelia," Shaw said. "Brandon, you see your work is clearly cut out for you there."

"Yes, sir," Brandon replied as he released his hold on me and stood up.

"Chloe and Fang, you can train independently."

They both nodded in understanding. Chloe started kicking at a punching bag while Fang settled onto the all-in-one weight training machine. Kelly and Ophelia set to work training on the mats on the opposite side of the room. Brandon cracked his knuckles before he began his lessons.

"Okay, so it's pretty safe to say you have no experience with this kind of stuff." It was a statement of fact, not a question. I nodded anyhow. He sighed and moved to stand behind me. "First, I'm going to teach you how to block, because that pathetic attempt you just made would just get you some broken bones in your arms and maybe your ribs."

"Is the lesson on how to do this or all the reasons why I suck at it?"

"Just listen." He grabbed my arms and positioned them so I was correctly blocking. "You want to keep your face behind your hands and your hands in fists. That way, you can punch when you get the opportunity and put your block back up quickly."

"I don't know how to punch anyone."

"We'll get to that." His fingers rested on top of mine from when he put my hands into proper fists, with my thumbs on top of my fingers instead of beneath them. Before I realized what was happening, he spun me around and swung at me. His fist connected with my forearm.

"Ow!"

"That was a decent block. Are you really going to say 'ow' every time I demonstrate something?"

I dropped my arms and cemented my hands to my hips. "Did you have to hit me as hard as you can?"

"Do you think the people who will be hunting you—yes, sweetheart, there are people who will be coming for you—are going to go easy on you because you're a girl?"

"Don't call me sweetheart," I hissed.

"Do you want to learn how to get out of trouble or not? It's not like you can just go around setting fires everywhere. That can't be your only method of defense!" His face was close to mine again. He had to crane his neck down to put his face that close. There was a predatory glint in his eyes, and something else that I couldn't put my finger on. My spine went rigid and my nerves got all prickly again.

I dropped my arms to my sides and stepped back from him. "Fine. We'll do it your way. I'm not interested in dying or being someone's slave."

He sighed and pinched the bridge of his nose between his thumb and index finger. "Punch me."

"What?" Incredulity colored my tone.

"Well, I have to see how crappy your punch is so I can correct it."

His body tensed, but only just slightly. He was expecting my punch to make little to no impact. I balled up my fist, closed my eyes, and swung as hard as I could. He sucked in a sharp breath when my fist made contact with him. When I opened my eyes, I saw that I hit him in the diaphragm. My eyes widened in shock. "I'm sorry!"

"That was a lucky hit," he wheezed. "If you want that success every time you have to watch what you're doing. If we were in a real fight and you closed your eyes, I would've just grabbed your wrist and snapped it. Punch me again."

The training session went on for hours. He taught me how to jab, how to block, how to throw a sucker punch, and to use our difference in height to my advantage. I snuck looks over at Ophelia and Kelly every once in a while. She was completely absorbed in learning hand to hand combat. She would do whatever it took to survive here. I needed to find that drive in myself. I couldn't help but feel a little lost in this new environment.

Kelly looked like a warrior when he demonstrated different things to Ophelia. His agility resembled a tiger's, graceful and fierce. Brandon looked like a cobra, confident in the knowledge that he could kill you with little effort. They were both beautiful to watch, in their own way. While I was distracted by my observations, Brandon's fist connected with the side of my eye, where my tattoos were. Bright colored spots winked over my vision before it just went black all together.

When I came to, Fang held Brandon up against the wall by the collar of his shirt and was yelling in his face. Chloe was punching Fang in the arm to no avail. Ophelia was trying to talk Fang down. Kelly was kneeling next to me, dabbing lightly at my eyebrow with a damp cloth. When he pulled it away from my face, small amounts of blood were soaked into it. My ears were ringing, so it was hard to understand what exactly was being said by whom.

Kelly's voice was the first one to come through clearly. "You took quite a hard hit, there."

I sat up slowly, the room spinning as I did. I shook my head back and forth gently to clear my brain. Brandon looked over at me. Fang followed his gaze, and when he saw I was sitting up—Kelly put his arm on my back to steady me—he dropped Brandon in a heap and came over to me. Ophelia followed suit, leaving Chloe to dote on her brother. He ignored her attentions and came over to me, too.

"Miss Sable, how are you feeling?" Fang's expression was full of concern.

"Dizzy," I mumbled.

"That's why you're supposed to pay attention when you're being taught." Brandon's tone was cold, but the concern in his eyes betrayed him. If looks could kill, Fang would have been guilty of murder.

"Is there anything we can do for you?" Kelly helped me stand and locked his arm around my waist, supporting my swaying body.

"Grilled cheese." I didn't know why, but that sounded amazing.

Kelly chuckled. "Let's get you back to your room. I think you've had enough training for this afternoon."

"I'll take her," Brandon offered.

"Like hell you will!" Fang protested.

"It's okay, Fang. He can apologize to me on the way back."

Brandon raised an eyebrow at the suggestion and replaced Kelly as my support. I didn't expect him to apologize, but I figured hearing me say I did would soothe Fang's nerves. Fang gave a stiff nod and Brandon led me out of the room.

When we turned the first corner on the way back to my room, Brandon took a deep breath and started speaking. "Look, Sable—"

"Don't. I don't care if you're going to apologize or lecture me or whatever, just save it." I gingerly touched my injured eye and winced. I could tell I'd have a black eye soon if I didn't already.

Brandon closed his mouth and we walked in silence the rest of the way.

When I was finally back in my room, I dared to look at my reflection in the mirror. A swirl of purple and blue made a backdrop for my tattoos. It looked kind of cool, but soon enough it would just look like I got punched in the face. I laughed without humor as I thought of what my parents' reaction to me having a black eye would be. I reminded myself that that didn't matter now.

I changed out of my clothes into a pair of pajamas I'd purchased on our shopping trip. It was a black ribbed tank top with a white skull and crossbones on it. The skull was adorned with a pink bow on the left side. Thin black cotton shorts, that had the same girly skull and crossbones, came with the tank. Just as I settled into my bed, a knock sounded on the door. With a frustrated groan, I padded to the door and threw it open.

To my surprise, Brandon stood on the other side of the door with a plate of grilled cheese in his hand. My jaw dropped as I stared from his face to the sandwich and back to his face.

"May I come in?" Still in shock, I nodded, unable to make the words leave my throat. He clicked the door closed behind him. I sat back down on my bed and he stood at the foot of it, handing the plate of grilled cheese to me. When I took it from him, I noticed it wasn't simply melted cheese between two slices of toasted bread. Like he'd read the question on my face, he said, "It's provolone and mozzarella cheese with diced tomatoes and pesto on sourdough."

I took a bite of the sandwich. It was delicious. "Who makes all this gourmet food here?"

His eyes were glued to the floor. "I do."

"Um, you can sit down if you want," I offered. I took another bite of the sandwich as he sat down next to me. Swallowing the tasty bite, I asked, "Where did you learn how to cook like this?"

"My dad was a chef, and when I was a kid, I couldn't learn enough about it. I wanted to be just like him. I had it all planned out that I was going to study in Paris as soon as I was old enough. Then I was going to open up a restaurant of my own, but I didn't know where. Then Chloe let it slip what she could do with water. It wasn't on purpose, but my parents freaked out. They didn't know what I could do with electricity. Anyhow, they were going to send her away, we didn't know where to. So in the middle of the night, we packed our stuff and took off. We were going to go to Paris. That was the plan, anyway. This ship was docked in the harbor, so we sneaked onto it. We sort of lucked out that Shaw is who he is and that he taught us how to use and control our abilities." Sadness fogged his eyes while he spoke of his past.

I stopped eating my sandwich and started chewing on my lip instead. I set the plate aside on the small table between mine and Ophelia's beds.

"That's how I ended up in the asylum. I was dreaming about setting things on fire and I almost burned my house down. My parents sent me away because they couldn't deal with having a freak for a daughter anymore." Subconsciously, my hand found its way over to Brandon's and settled on top of it. He looked down at my hand and twined our fingers together tentatively.

"Brandon…"

With his other hand, he traced the edges of my bruise. A pang of guilt flashed over his features but disappeared quickly, his stoic mask returning. His fingertips brushed lightly down my cheek, and then his hand cupped my jaw. He titled my head up to his and pressed his lips against mine. I blinked in surprise. My free hand grabbed on to the back of his neck, pulling him closer to me.

For a moment he caved, his kisses becoming hungrier as he sucked my bottom lip into his mouth. A groan sounded low in his throat. His hand left my jaw and latched onto the small of my back, pressing me against him. My grip tightened on his hand that I still held. Suddenly, he disconnected from me, stood, and left the room without a word or a backward glance. He took all the oxygen left in my lungs with him.

How bizarre was he? I fell back onto my bed and closed my eyes. His fevered kisses still burned on my lips as I drifted off to sleep.

IX

My head was throbbing when I woke up. Ophelia sat on her bed, crocheting something that was unrecognizable at the present moment. I brushed my lips with my fingertips, the memory of Brandon's lips on mine immediately present in my conscious mind. Ophelia noticed me stir and put her crocheting project aside. She settled next to me on my bed.

"How's your eye?"

"It hurts," I croaked while I sat up. I drew my knees up to my chest and hugged them close to me. "Does it look awful?"

"It's pretty apparent," she mused.

"Damn."

"Well, he did hit you pretty hard. Fang was about to rip his arm out of the socket." A small smile played on her lips as she got lost in the memory of Fang's outrage.

"He's like the brother I never had."

"He's not old enough to be your father, anyhow. He's only ten years older than me, and I'm eighteen."

"Really? That makes me feel really young." I had a flash-back of being at a family reunion and being the youngest one there. My parents had me later in their lives, after they were well established in their careers. All my cousins were at least ten years older than me. I hated that I never had anyone to re-late to when I went to family functions.

"How old are you?"

"Sixteen."

"Same as Chloe. Brandon and Kelly are both seventeen. They're closer to being the right age to be like biological brothers to you."

I would never do with someone I considered my brother what I'd just done with Brandon.

"How long was I asleep?"

She shrugged. "Well, I've been in here for about an hour. You came in here about an hour and a half before that."

That meant it was somewhere around early evening. I wondered what everyone else was doing. Ophelia wasn't a terribly social person, it seemed, so if the rest of them were all doing something together, she might not be the one to ask about it. Although, if Fang was still mad about Brandon punching me, he probably wouldn't be in the mood to be so-cializing either.

A knock sounded at the door. Ophelia put her hand on my shoulder, telling me to stay put, and went to open it. Kelly stood on the other side.

"It's time for dinner." He gave a polite smile and clasped his hand behind his back. "If you ladies are interested."

"Sable needs to get dressed first, and then we'll join you."

"I'll just wait out here, then."

Ophelia swung the door shut and looked at me. "You have to eat something. I saw that you barely ate your grilled cheese sandwich before you passed out."

"Yeah. I guess I just didn't feel like eating right then." Not to mention I was distracted.

I climbed out of bed and went to the closet. I pulled out a pair of red, black, and white plaid pants with two black straps that crossed over the backs of my legs and a black, hooded, knit sweater that had buckles on the wrists with slightly belled sleeves and three safety pins on both sides just under my collar bone. I zipped the sweater up to my chest and pulled my pants on over my shorts. When she was satisfied that I was completely dressed, Ophelia opened the door. Kelly was standing with his back to it like a bodyguard.

"Lead on," Ophelia said as I shut the door behind us.

Kelly jumped a little in surprise and turned around to look at us. He offered me a weak smile as he eyed my bruise then led us toward what I assumed would be a dining room.

When we arrived, Shaw, Brandon, and Chloe were already eating. Fang sat with an empty plate, waiting for us to arrive. Four thick white squares of fish prepared blackened style sat on a platter and a bowl of mixed greens tossed in an opaque yellowish dressing sat beside it.

As Ophelia and I sat down, Kelly put a piece of fish and about a handful of salad on our plates. Fang, apparently, had to serve himself. A glass of white wine was served to each person with their meal. I looked at my glass skeptically. I'd never drunk good wine before, just the stuff that came in boxes you could get for cheap. *You might as well have chugged down some rubbing alcohol and saved yourself eight dollars.*

"What, you don't drink?" The accusation came from Chloe.

I didn't know she'd been paying me any attention, let alone noticed that I was in the room. I wasn't sure what answer she was looking for, so I just focused on eating my fish.

It was heavier than I'd expected it to be. Most of the fish I'd had experience with—which wasn't many—was light and flaky. While the flavor of the fish was delicate, it was texturally heavy like beef steak.

Like he was reading my thoughts, Kelly asked, "Have you ever had swordfish before?"

"You can eat swordfish?"

Chloe snorted. "You just did, didn't you?"

My cheeks flushed as I focused my attention on my plate again.

"What's all on the menu tonight, Brandon?" Kelly ignored the tension in the room and tried being jovial.

"Blackened swordfish, bitter greens tossed in a light balsamic dressing, and you're drinking chardonnay." Brandon didn't seem particularly excited about his meal.

As I continued to eat, I only half tasted everything. Brandon definitely inherited his father's talent for cooking, but I was thinking more about Brandon than his food. The rest of the meal was eaten in silence. When Shaw was finished, he gave Brandon and Kelly training instructions for the next day and then left the table. One by one as we finished our meals, people departed from the dining room. I was the last one to finish, only half my meal consumed. I felt bad about wasting the food, but I couldn't seem to interest myself in eating.

It took a little longer than I'd expected to wander back to my room. At least, that's where I expected to be going. Instead, I wound up on the ship's deck. The sea air was chilly and smelled like salty fish. I leaned against the railing and then slid down to sit on the deck. A low rumbling sounded in the sky. It was going to rain.

As the drops started falling, I hugged my knees close to my chest and looked up at the storm clouds. It felt like a light summer rain shower, but I knew how quickly it could turn into a downpour. Since it was only drizzling, I drew pictures in the air in front of me with fire. I was nowhere near an artist, but I'd always found myself doodling when I was bored in school. As soon as I'd finish a picture, it would drown into a smoky shadow of the bright orange it started as. When the raindrops got fatter, I pulled the hood on my sweater over my head. It wouldn't keep me dry for long.

"That's impressive." Kelly sat down next to me and tucked his glasses in his shirt so they wouldn't get spotted from the rain.

I hugged my knees tighter to my chest. "I didn't know anyone was watching."

"I wasn't spying, I promise. I actually had a proposition for you."

I rested my head on top of my knees and looked at him. His profile made his cheekbones stand out. "What kind of proposition?"

"It was Ophelia's idea, actually. If you wanted to train with me instead of Brandon tomorrow, we'd understand."

"We who?"

"Ophelia and me I guess." He closed his eyes and tried to smooth out the grimace on his face.

"No one asked Brandon about it?"

"No."

"Well, I appreciate the offer, Kelly, but I don't want Brandon to feel bad about all this. Accidents happen. If I'd been paying attention, I could've ducked or spun out of the way or something." I brushed my hair into my face, trying to hide the bruise from view.

"That's very noble of you." Kelly stood then and offered his hand to me. It was starting to rain harder still, so I took it. He helped me stand and then escorted me back to my room.

When I clicked the door shut, I found Ophelia asleep on her bed. I peeled off my pants and my sweater and crawled into bed. Sleep didn't come as easily as I would've liked.

ဢၵၵ

Training the next week was awkward, to say the least. Everyone's eyes were on Brandon and me as if they were afraid he would explode into a violent fit or something. Instead of having me use him as punching bag, he had me use a real one. He showed me how to kick someone like I was striking them in the kneecaps. When he kicked the bag, it swayed back and forth. When I kicked it, it didn't budge.

"Maybe we should have you weight train first," he muttered after about an hour of me attacking the punching bag and getting nowhere. Sweat poured off of me. I'd never done anything this physical before, unless you counted gym class. This was like gym class on steroids, but without playing any team sports. I almost asked when he was going to make me climb a rope, but when I saw a rope dangling from the ceiling, I thought better of it.

When he was satisfied that I was exhausted, he brought me to the ship's deck and had me run laps. At first, my lungs burned and my muscles ached. By the end of the week, I guess I started showing some promise since Shaw came to watch me train. After I finished running laps, I stood next to Brandon and waited for Shaw's assessment. The sun reflected off Brandon's tanned skin and made it seem like he was glowing.

"Keep this training going. I want you to start adding weapons." Then Shaw turned his attention to me. "Hopefully you'll manage not to get yourself cut up. I'll start training you to harness your fire power. Your eye looks better, by the way."

With that, he left us standing on the deck. Brandon crossed his arms over his chest and looked at me. "You did good."

"Thanks, I guess…" An uncomfortable tension was thick between us. I took a deep breath before I spoke again. "Look, can we just start over or something? Forget you decked me, forget you kissed me, and maybe we can be friends? At least maybe being colleagues will be less awkward."

"You want me to forget we kissed?" He sounded surprised. His eyebrows shot up to his hairline.

"Well, I know how it is. You do something you don't mean to do and then it's all weird afterwards because you wish you could take it back, but you can't."

"Do you want to forget it happened?" His voice was quiet, his eyes hard as diamonds.

A blush blossomed in my cheeks as I stared down at the deck. My voice was so quiet, I barely heard myself speak. "No."

Then I felt his hand settle on the small of my back. "Come on, let's get you cleaned up. You're going to be exhausted tomorrow."

"Like I'm not already," I grumbled.

He chuckled at that and walked below deck with me.

When I got back to our room, Ophelia was just stepping out of the shower. Her hair was wrapped up in a towel and she donned a fluffy bathrobe.

"So what did Shaw have to say?" Ophelia definitely knew how to cut to the chase.

"He said I'm supposed to start training with weapons and that he's going to train me how to use my fire power better." I sat on the edge of my bed, not wanting my sweat to soak into it.

"I got a similar report." She was practically beaming. "That means we're progressing."

"I guess it's a good thing we're learning to defend ourselves. I wish we knew how to do that when we were at the asylum."

"It wouldn't have done much good. Fang knows how to fight. When they first brought him down, he fought back hard. It didn't matter how many times they came at him, he'd throw up a shield and block them. They had enough orderlies to take him on until he was exhausted. When he collapsed, it was brutal. They wouldn't stop beating him. Even when he was bleeding, they kept going. After he was completely broken, Doctor Pantiel called them off." As she recounted the story, her face leeched of color. I guessed mine had, too. I felt sick to my stomach and had the sudden urge to go find Fang and hug him.

"At least we're here now." It was a poor attempt to console her, but it seemed to do some good.

While she started putting on her pajamas, I hopped into the shower. I was eager to get to sleep, but I was nervous about training with Shaw. He had a certain intensity about him that made me want to fidget beneath his gaze.

When I slept that night, I dreamed about fighting with weapons and being good at it. I brandished a flaming sword and cut down all the faceless foes in my path. The dream me was much more agile and graceful than the real me. When I woke up, I was slightly disappointed. I liked seeing myself as a fearless warrior. Maybe by the end of my training, I would be.

X

I smoothed the pleats down on my yellow, red, and black plaid mini skirt as I waited for Shaw in his office and stared out the windows into the ocean. Miscellaneous schools of dark colored fish swam by, unaware of the foreign object in the middle of their home. Sometimes a shark would swim past. The view was more impressive than any aquarium I'd ever seen.

The door swung open with a creaking noise, and heavy footsteps sounded in the room behind me. I didn't bother turning around to see who it was. I knew it would be Shaw. He appeared in front of me on the other side of his desk. Ignoring me, he shuffled through some papers and then set to work scribbling a note on a pad. After he finished organizing it all, he turned his attention to me.

"I'll say I'm surprised you've made it this far. I don't think I've ever had a...pupil...take a hit like that. Most of the people that have come through this way are a lot less rough around the edges." He sat with his hands folded on top of his desk while he spoke.

"Tell me how you really feel," I muttered.

He scowled. "Brandon neglected to tell me about that mouth of yours, however."

I cast my eyes downward into my lap. "Sorry."

"Enough. We didn't come here to talk about your lack of prerequisites. So is that all you can do is start miniature fires on whim?"

"I just learned how to do that recently. Fang helped me with it. Before that, they just seemed to happen at random."

His expression was filled with curiosity. "How did you know you were the cause of the fires, then?"

"One day I was thinking about something being on fire, and then it was."

He tapped his index finger on his chin, a pensive light to his eyes. "And the only way you produce fire is from your mind?"

"I can make it appear in my hands, too." I drew a flame out of fire in the air between us. That seemed like the best way to demonstrate my point.

"What about the rest of you?"

"What do you mean?"

"You've seen how Brandon can course electricity throughout his body, haven't you?" I nodded. "Can you do that with fire?"

"I've never tried."

"Well, stand up and try it now."

"I don't want to burn anything."

Shaw snorted. "You're afraid of leaving scorch marks on the floor? Who says you'll even make the flames extend that far?"

I stood from my chair and walked to the center of the open space in the room, then I squeezed my eyes shut in concentration. My fingers started to tingle as I focused on producing flames from them. When my hands felt significantly warmer, I knew there were flames coming from them. I envisioned the flames traveling up my arms to my shoulders, then spreading up my neck and down my body. I couldn't tell if I started sweating because of the warmth of the flames or because I was concentrating so hard. I quickly became fatigued, and the flames stopped at my torso before I nearly collapsed.

All of a sudden, I felt much colder and started panting. I put my hands on my knees to brace myself since I felt a little lightheaded. The feeling reminded me of the first time Brandon pushed me to sprint laps around the deck. I opened my eyes and glanced up at Shaw, who watched me with an expressionless face. The man would've made an excellent poker player.

"Do it again." A command, not a request.

"I don't—know if I—can," I said between gasps.

"I never said this would be comfortable."

"Are you trying—to make—me pass out?"

"Perhaps." His face gave away nothing.

With an aggravated sigh, I concentrated again on producing fire from my hands. I didn't make it as far as the last time. My knees gave out and I collapsed on the floor. My hands were shaking from exertion. Sweat dripped from my neck down my spine. Shaw got up from his chair and knelt in front of me. He lifted my chin with his hand so I was looking into his eyes.

"You're supposed to get better, not worse. Do it again and push yourself. Don't fear your strength, embrace it." His eyes were fierce but not menacing.

I took a deep breath and tried one more time. Still on my knees, I pushed the flames up to the top of my head, my hair turning into flaming whips. I pushed the fire down my torso to my thighs, but it was too much. The flames burned off slowly, but I felt like my brain had been turned to mush.

"Stop rushing and do it again. Concentrate." He still knelt in front of me, his intense energy inspiring me to try again.

The burn sizzled over my skin as I pushed the flames up and down my body at an agonizingly slow rate. I gritted my teeth together as a growl sounded low in my throat.

"Open your eyes," Shaw instructed.

I watched as the flames crawled across my skin and my clothes. It was sort of amazing that the fabric didn't burn away. The flames enveloped my knees and started towards my calves. I was excited that I'd been able to push myself that far, but my energy was quickly draining away. My chest heaved with every breath I managed. I felt my heart slow in my chest. Any moment now and I'd lose consciousness.

"Stop." The word sounded fuzzy and far away in my ears, the sound of my pulse thundering in my head drowning it out. "Bring the flames back to your hands. Draw them back into you."

I almost felt like crying. He was asking too much. My stomach lurched as my lightheadedness intensified. I watched the flames disappear from my legs. The ends of my hair turned from fiery whips to chocolate brown tresses.

Somewhere between the time the flames left my torso and the time they left my upper arms, I blacked out. Since I was still upright, it couldn't have been for that long. When the fire finally, blessedly, extinguished in my palms, my whole body was racked with tremors. Everything felt like gelatin.

"That's more than I expected from you. I'll have Brandon escort you back to your room." Shaw helped me get to my feet and over to the chair, which I ungracefully flopped into.

I wasn't sure how much time passed before Brandon was there to walk me back to my room. Shaw helped me over to his office door and I stumbled the whole way there. As Brandon took my arm, Shaw instructed him to send Ophelia to his office for her bout of training. I imagined we would both be passed out for a while after these training sessions.

After the first few stumbled steps down the hall, Brandon picked me up, one arm slung beneath my knees and the other around my lower back. His hands rested on my thigh and my waist.

The heat on my skin from his touch was somehow hotter than the heat of the fire. My cheeks flushed as I allowed my head to rest against his chest. My hands were still shaking, but I wasn't so sure exhaustion was the catalyst anymore.

"How did you do?" His interest seemed only mild.

"Good I guess. Better than Shaw expected, anyway."

"That's because I trained you." I could tell he was smirking even though I wasn't looking at his face.

"You didn't teach me to use fire."

He chuckled as we rounded the corner into the hallway my room was in. When we stopped in front of my door, Brandon kicked it. Ophelia opened the door, a cross expression on her face until she realized I was being carried.

"Sable, what happened?" she gasped. Then she looked reproachfully at Brandon, probably assuming he did something to me.

"I feel like my bones melted."

"Shaw wants to see you for training in his office. That's where Sable came from." He kept his tone even, but the way his body became rigid when he spoke implied he was aggravated with the unspoken accusation. With a nod to Brandon and a sympathetic smile to me, Ophelia departed to meet with Shaw.

Brandon carried me over to my bed and set me down on it gently. Then he sat down next to me and stretched out. My head was close to his chest. I rolled over on my side and curled my legs up a little, like when I was falling asleep. I breathed in the scent of his skin. He smelled like anise and lemongrass. It was bright and reminded me of springtime.

Then I felt his fingertips graze my cheekbone as he brushed a lock of hair off of my face and hooked it behind my ear. Even though my skin felt hot, it broke out in goose bumps. I tilted my head so I could look into his eyes. He stared back into mine, an unreadable expression on his face. I found myself holding my breath, although I didn't know what for. He slid his fingers beneath mine and lifted my hand to his lips. He kissed my knuckles, each one in turn, then each of my fingertips, then the inside of my wrist. My pulse hammered against his mouth.

A tiny moan escaped as my lips parted. He looked back into my eyes, his lips still pressed to my wrist. His name floated from me on a breathy sigh.

"Again," he said softly. My brow puckered in confusion. "My name. Say it again."

"Brandon." The second half of the word was swallowed up by his mouth connecting with mine. Something about him gave me strength, and I found myself cupping his face in my hands. Then he pulled me onto his lap. Our lips, tongues, and teeth banged together in reckless abandon. His hands gripped tightly around my waist as I fisted a hand in his hair. My name came out as a groan and I swallowed the sound.

He pulled me closer to him until there was no space between our chests. Our breaths were ragged. Need coursed through my veins, hot and intense. Brandon pulled us down on the bed so that I was lying on top of him. I broke away from him and caught my breath. My hands were cemented on his chest as I stared at his face. His black locks were as wild as his eyes, which moved from my face down to my navel and then back up to meet my eyes. He was breathing hard, just like me.

Then a knock sounded at the door.

Brandon cursed under his breath and moved me gently off of him. He sat up and raked a hand through his disheveled hair. The knocking came again.

"Yes?" I gasped.

"Sable? Are you all right?" It was Kelly.

I swallowed and replied with more vibrato. "Yes."

Having regained his composure, Brandon went to the door and opened it.

"Oh, Brandon. I didn't expect you to be here." Kelly shifted from one foot to the other as he looked from Brandon to me.

"I was escorting her back to her room, as per Shaw's instructions."

"Yes, and he was offering to make me some french toast," I added quickly.

Brandon looked over his shoulder at me, his brow puckered in confusion. My eyes widened and I raised my eyebrows, willing him to just go with it. He looked back to Kelly and muttered something about french toast as he walked out of the room.

"May I come in?" Kelly asked.

I nodded, and he came in. His soft brown eyes were filled with concern.

"Does Shaw need me for something?"

"No, no. Nothing like that. Ophelia reported to Fang and me that your training session had been particularly strenuous. I just wanted to make sure you were all right." He sat down on the bed next to me.

"I'm fine now." I sat cross-legged, resting my elbows on my shins and my chin in my hands.

"Please don't take this the wrong way, but you seem sort of…delicate."

"No, I get it." I sighed. I was really becoming motivated to be the best woman warrior on this ship.

"Would you like your dinner brought to you in your room?"

"I think Brandon's bringing me french toast, but thanks."

He smiled and then leaned over and kissed my cheek, lingering for just a moment before he pulled away. I blinked in surprise, making him grin. He pushed his glasses farther up the bridge of his nose as he left the room.

It was odd, the difference between Brandon and Kelly's kisses. Kelly made me feel comforted, like he would always take care of everything. Brandon's kisses left my nerve endings tingling, sensitive to the lightest touch.

I yearned for Ophelia to come back so I had someone to talk to about this. My fingers traced over my lips and then slid to my cheek, touching where someone else's lips had been. I slumped back onto the mattress with a sigh. I could already tell disaster was imminent.

XI

A short while later, someone knocked on the door. I dragged myself out of bed and over to the door. I didn't feel like I had the energy to deal with anyone right then. When Fang turned out to be the one on the other side, I was relieved. He held a covered plate in his hand.

"Come in!" I almost squealed. Fang smiled and walked into the room behind me. He wouldn't walk ahead of me out of respect. When I sat back down on the bed, he handed the plate over to me. "What's for dinner?"

"Well, Miss Sable, we all had shrimp jambalaya. Brandon made you bananas foster french toast."

I lifted off the cover to find delicate looking french toast triangles adorned with bananas and a sort of caramel sauce. A fork rested on the side of the plate. I seized it and savored the richly sweet meal. "Do you want a bite? This is amazing!"

Fang chuckled. "I done had my fill."

As I tried not to inhale the rest of my meal, Fang sat quietly on the edge of Ophelia's bed. He looked healthier than when I first met him. I guessed we all did. Ophelia and I didn't look so sallow, and she was filling into her natural curvaceous figure. I imagined that when she got back to her normal size, she'd have a perfect hourglass figure that would leave any man drooling behind her.

When I finished eating, I set the plate down on the bedside table and sat next to Fang. Before I knew quite what I was doing, I threw my arms around him. My hands didn't quite touch to completely encircle him. His chest was too broad. His strong arms banded around me and he laid his head on top of mine. "I missed you so much, Fang."

"I'm just across the hall, Miss Sable, whenever you want to see me." Then he held me at arm's length and looked me over. "You're looking much better than when we first met. And that bruise by your eye is almost gone, too. If I thought you looked lovely before, you're quite something now."

"Fang! Stop it! Don't make me blush!"

It was too late for that, however. Fang chuckled and tousled the hair on top of my head, like I was his little sister. I'd always wanted siblings, but my parents always insisted I was enough for them. My heart panged uncomfortably at the thought.

"All right now, you need to be getting some rest. We're all in for an intense day tomorrow. Shaw's got big plans for all six of us, so he says. I hope I can show him what I can really do. And I'd love to see you take those boys on. I really think you can give them a run for their money." He winked and took the empty plate from the table. Before he left, he bid me goodnight and kissed me on the forehead.

I changed into my pajamas and slid into bed. My pillows still smelled of anise and lemongrass. A shadow of a smile played on my lips as I fell asleep.

The next morning, when I woke up I felt revitalized. A nervous sort of tension hung in the air as Ophelia and I dressed for the day. I wore a black fitted T-shirt that had the word "punk" written on it in sparkling pink letters, with a large silver safety pin stitched above the text, and a pair of electric blue and purple zebra striped skinny jeans with black gladiator style sandals. Ophelia donned a bright orange tutu with black leggings beneath it and a white spaghetti strapped shirt with a three quarter sleeved denim jacket and lime green high heels. As we walked out the door, I hastily fastened my hair into low slung pig tails.

Fang met us in the hallway. He dressed in Army-issued camouflage pants and an Army green utility vest with heavy tan workman's boots. We traded pleasantries as we walked to the training room. Upon our arrival, Brandon, Chloe, and Kelly were waiting outside the door. Brandon stood with a regal air, despite his baggy jeans, oversized gray T-shirt, and black skateboarding sneakers.

Chloe brandished brown leather mini shorts with a black leather gun holster strapped across her hips, a cream bustier, a coffee colored leather duster, and above-the-knee cream-colored suede stiletto boots with brass buckles across the ankles, and a pair of brass-rimmed goggles perched on top of her head.

Kelly wore khaki pants, a button up pale yellow long sleeved shirt with the sleeves pushed up to his elbows, and white sneakers. We definitely didn't look like the sort of people who would be assembled together.

"Why are we waiting out here?" I asked no one in particular.

Brandon crossed his arms over his chest as a scowl formed on his face. "There's a CIA agent inside, and Shaw's conferencing with him before we have to make an exhibition of our skills."

"Why is the CIA here?" I was more confused than uneasy, although they were starting to be more evenly matched.

"They check in on us every once in a while and we give them a show to save face. When they're satisfied we're not plotting against the government, they leave and we go back to our routine," Kelly explained.

We all settled into an uncomfortable silence. I tried in vain to hear what Shaw and the CIA agent were talking about, but I couldn't hear a thing. After a long while passed, Shaw opened the door and motioned with a single wave of his hand for us to follow him inside. We walked single file, Brandon in front and Fang in the rear with the rest of us shuffled in between.

Shaw's desk chair was brought up from his office for the CIA agent to sit in. He stood up as we came into the room and stood in a straight line before him. He was a couple inches shorter than Shaw, with hair so blond it was almost white. He wore a black suit jacket and pants with a crisp white shirt, black neck tie, and black dress shoes.

I half expected for a pair of stylish black sunglasses to be concealing his dull green eyes, but there weren't any to be seen.

"Agent Casper, let me introduce you to my students. The first is Brandon Harper, aged seventeen, with the power of electrical currents. Next to him is his sister, Chloe Harper, aged sixteen, with the power to control water. Then is Ophelia Reinhardt, aged eighteen, with the gift of the sight of the future. Next is Kelly Anderson, aged seventeen, with the power of telekinesis. This is Sable Mosley, aged sixteen, with the power of fire. Lastly is Timothy 'Fang' Weston, aged twenty-eight, with the ability to produce kinetic shields."

As Shaw listed us off, Agent Casper stared each of us down in turn, as if he was trying to assess how lethal we were and how quickly he could take us out.

"Now we will demonstrate each student's unique abilities as well as their hand to hand combat skills," Shaw continued.

Without being prompted, Brandon stepped up to the first in a line of dummies and began punching and kicking it. Every blow he landed would've been lethal to a real person. Then Shaw snapped his fingers and Brandon picked up a heavy looking sword.

To my surprise, the dummy started fighting back with crude movements. He hacked and slashed away at the dummy, leaving deep gashes with stuffing protruding from them. Then his whole body lit up, and the electricity coursed through his body to his sword. He struck the final blow, slicing off the dummy's head, causing the mechanical parts of the dummy to seize, which left the dummy a crumpled mess on the floor.

Shaw snapped his fingers again and Brandon was replaced with Chloe. She was faster than Brandon, but not always as accurate, her hair a streaking flame around her face. Her kicks would spring her off the ground and high into the air, which was an amazing feat to accomplish in stilettos. While she continued launching herself at the dummy, Shaw produced a small bowl of water and placed it next to Agent Casper.

When she noticed it was there, Chloe turned her attention away from the dummy, whose mechanical components had been triggered to life. She put her hands together, arms outstretched towards the bowl. As she lifted her hands up over her head, the water in the bowl rose into the air. When she spread her hands apart, the mass of water stretched and became bigger.

She lowered the large floating orb of water over the dummy, showing that she could drown it if it were alive. Then she transferred the water back to the bowl and pulled a pistol out of the holster on her hip. She fired off three shots: one passed through the dummy's stomach, one passed through its heart, and one passed through its brain.

Ophelia punched and kicked at her dummy, but with less force than Brandon and slightly better accuracy than Chloe. She looked apprehensive as she landed blow after blow on her nonliving target. When she brandished her daggers, she found her confidence. She ripped the dummy apart, leaving only a crude skeleton of mechanical parts scattered on the floor. Then she threw the daggers down so they stuck into the floor.

She approached Agent Casper, and when she was about two paces away from him, she stood very still. I could picture the dead look in her eyes as her conscious mind left the present and travelled into the future.

After about five minutes, she said, "Tomorrow, Agent Casper, you will receive a phone call that someone has broken into Area 51 and stolen documentation about the Diseased."

"Ms. Reinhardt, there is no such thing as Area 51," Agent Casper replied coolly. His face showed no sign of whether or not he believed her.

"There is also no such thing as the Diseased, yet here we stand before you."

With that, she took her place back in line with the rest of us. While his expression remained the same, the agent's posture was more rigid than it had been.

Kelly had all the grace of a tiger as he assaulted his dummy. It was beautiful to watch, really. Every motion was fluid and blended from one to the next. His body was in a constant state of motion until he stopped to retrieve his weapon. He looked over at the wall of weapons, and a pair of sais floated toward him. When they were within his reach, he grabbed them and his dummy sprang to life. He used the sais to block the dummy's attacks and to stab into it. When the dummy clattered to the floor, he used his telekinesis to return it to its upright position.

Then it was my turn. I swallowed the lump in my throat as I attacked the dummy, just like Brandon showed me. When I was training, Brandon usually had me wear a pair of brass knuckles because he said I didn't hit very hard and it would aid me in causing some damage. I didn't have them now. I threw all my weight into every punch and kick. The dummy wobbled slightly when I connected with it. Then I grabbed up the whip Brandon was training me to use.

The dummy came to life as I cracked the whip on the floor, the sound reverberating through the room. I concentrated on fire appearing in my palm and snaking its way down the whip. I wasn't confident enough in my control of the flames yet to let them consume me like Brandon did with the electricity. The dummy lunged for me, and I wrapped its arms in my flaming whip, causing the fabric to burn. It didn't burn quickly like I hoped it would.

The more I kept hitting the dummy with the whip, the more it burned, until the fire hit the stuffing beneath the surface fabric and it exploded into large fire. Chloe quickly used the water from the bowl to extinguish the flames.

Fang fought like a tank, bulldozing over everything in his path. He didn't need a weapon— he was his own weapon. His physical attack was by far the strongest of all of us. His dummy was in motion from the start.

He used his kinetic shields to block its attacks and then struck back with his own. Then he punched the dummy square in the chest and knocked it into the wall. A loud crack rang out as the dummy's mechanical components broke apart inside it.

It flopped ungracefully to the floor as Fang took his place back in line.

After a few moments of jotting down notes in a notepad he kept in the breast pocket inside his jacket, Agent Casper addressed us. "Overall, it was very impressive. Shaw has been doing well with you. Perhaps too well. We'll check back on your progress, possibly in a few weeks, or maybe in a few months."

Without another word, he showed himself out, Shaw trailing behind him. The rest of us stood where we were.

"I hate when they come," Chloe grumbled.

I took my hair out of their pigtails and shook the strands loose. "It didn't seem so bad to me."

"Wait until Shaw comes back. He always finds flaws in our performances. Then we have to train like crazy until he settles down." She settled into a squat and adjusted the goggles on her head, which had been knocked askew when she was fighting.

As if Chloe summoned him by speaking his name, Shaw reappeared in the training room. She popped back up to a standing position and crossed her arms over her chest.

"You all have a lot of work ahead of you," he warned.

A collective groan sounded from everyone but Fang. I noticed that since we came here, he almost lived in this room on the home gym machine.

"Brandon, you need to work on speed. Chloe, you need sharper accuracy. Ophelia, you need more hand to hand combat training. Kelly, your weapons should be extensions of you, not something to slow down your attacks. Sable, you need weight training. Fang, your footwork needs attention. I want Brandon to train Ophelia, I want Kelly to train Sable, and I want Chloe to work with Fang. Now go!"

We broke off into our assigned pairs, and Kelly and I headed towards the weight training station. I looked over my shoulder at Brandon, whose gaze was fixed on Kelly. I turned my attention back to the weights. Kelly picked up a pair of ten pound dumbbells and handed them to me. "Take one in each hand and I'll show you how to do curls to work on your biceps. When they burn too much, we'll work on your triceps. Tomorrow we'll work on your legs and your core."

He grabbed a pair of forty pound dumbbells and showed me the proper techniques for each of the exercises he wanted me to do. He kept an eye on my progress while he worked with his sais, trying to make the motions more fluid like Shaw wanted him to do. The blades were held low in his hands so the handles pressed up into his forearms. Gradually, he gripped more and more of the handle until he was holding them properly.

My muscles screamed with each repetition of exercises I did, so I put the weights down. Kelly was still working with his sais. It looked like he was dragging them through water. Then a thought struck me. I made a fire in my hands and blended it with the air—like I used my palms to blend in my rouge when I used too much.

A flat rectangular-shaped red-and-orange square flickered in the air. Kelly seemed to understand what I was trying to do with it, and he slashed at the rectangle until it looked like flaming ribbons floating in the air. As the fire turned to smoke, he smiled at me through the haze.

"That was a good idea."

"I thought it might help to have something tangible but that wouldn't offer any resistance for you to cut through so you could tell how smooth or choppy your movements were."

Brandon walked over to us. "Kelly, I thought you were supposed to be training her, not the other way around."

"And what of your training Ophelia, then?" A smile was still on his lips, but his eyes betrayed the sentiment. His male pride was bruised a little.

"She's carrying on without me. I'm off to make dinner." He started to turn away and paused. His eyes locked with mine for a few brief moments before he seemed to remember he was leaving.

I stared after the confounding boy, who left the room, running his hands through his shaggy black locks as he went.

XII

A week after Agent Casper came for the assessment, Shaw received an invitation for the seven of us to come to some fundraising event or something like that. It was at the White House, and we were provided with funds to purchase more appropriate attire, with a note that stressed it was a black tie function.

We docked on the coast of Maryland and set off to acquire suitable tuxedos and gowns. I chose a floor length red silk, long-sleeved, backless dress that hugged my minimal curves and had a neckline that rested just under my collar bone. I wore strappy black cage stilettos, but you could only see the very bottom of the spike heel beneath the hem of the dress.

Chloe picked a Victorian style gown with a high neck and long sleeves. The bodice of the dress was white, with a full violet skirt and a black corset to synch in her already tiny waist and a large black feather in her hair, which was pulled up into an elegant French twist. Black leather stiletto boots which buttoned up the back completed the look.

Ophelia chose a one-sleeved, mermaid silhouette, royal blue dress made of satin which she wore with glittering gold heels.

The night of the event, we were escorted from our hotel to the White House by limousine. Once we arrived, we waited in a long line of limousines to be let out on a red carpet which led to the entry. As we got closer to our destination, the many flashes from the hordes of paparazzi and various news stations reporters made a strobe light effect. The indiscernible figures making their way down the red carpet paused at random intervals to pose for pictures and to speak with the reporters and journalists.

As we finally stepped out of our limo, the camera flashes temporarily blinded me, causing me to stumble a bit over my dress. Kelly steadied me by placing one hand on my upper arm and the other on the small of my back. I gave him a grateful smile, which he returned, as he offered his arm to me. He looked quite handsome in his black tuxedo.

All the men at this function were wearing the same thing with small variations: black tuxedos, some with tails, some without, a black bowtie, a crisp white shirt, a black cummerbund, and shiny black dress shoes. Some donned top hats, but no one I arrived with did. Their tuxedos were all exactly the same. Fang was going to wear a white tuxedo, but Shaw opposed idea with vehemence.

Shaw was walking the farthest ahead. Behind him, Brandon escorted Chloe He had his hair slicked back so just the ends of it curled under. In front of Kelly and me, Fang escorted Ophelia

At the door to the White House, security guards used a metal detecting wand to ensure none of us, or any of the other party guests, were carrying any weapons. Once we'd all been inspected, we followed the crowd to the ball room where the festivities had already begun. A small orchestra played soft music that seemed to float in the air over the party guests. People milled around and chatted with one another. Waiters weaved in between the guests with trays of champagne flutes filled with bubbling liquid and hors d'oeuvres. A few couples danced on a mid-sized rectangle of floor near the orchestra.

Our group remained huddled together, unsure of why we'd been summoned here. The impression I got from the atmosphere told me that this was a party for wealthy diplomats. None of us fit into that category. Tension pulled the muscles in my neck and shoulders taut. I picked at the end of one of the curls that spilled down from my elaborate up do.

The curls in my hair twisted around each other, creating a web of chocolate ropes that all gathered on the crown of my head and were fastened with pins with pearls on the ends of them. A few hung loose to frame my face, and a couple fell over my left shoulder.

Kelly smiled at me and eyed the dance floor. My nose scrunched up in confusion, which caused him to chuckle. As he held his hand out to me, he asked, "May I have this dance?"

I didn't know how to dance, really, but I didn't want to be rude and decline the invitation. I found myself nodding and he escorted me to the dance floor.

Dancing with Kelly was easier than I'd expected it to be. He swept me around the dance floor with all the grace and skill of a professional. The orchestra played a waltz, and we glided over the floor. I knew I wasn't doing the right steps and was thankful no one could see my feet beneath my dress. A blush blossomed on my cheeks as I realized people had begun watching us. Even some of the other dancing couples stopped to watch.

Kelly took that as an invitation to use more of the floor space. When the song ended, he spun me in a slow turn while the onlookers clapped like they would at a golf game.

"You're not half bad you know," he said with a smile.

In spite of myself, I smiled, too. "Just because you're so good. You didn't tell me you could dance."

"I'd practice with my mother. It was a hobby of hers, dancing. Sometimes my father would take her out to dance. He wasn't great at it, but she never told him that. She thought it was sweet that he tried, I guess." Kelly's eyes looked wistful as he spoke. Then he focused on me again as the orchestra started playing a new song, this one more up tempo. "Come on, let's have a little fun."

As we spun around the dance floor, the rest of the room became a blur. He held me by my right hand and the small of my back. Sometimes, he'd throw in extra little twirls or some fancy footwork, which caused the onlookers to ooh and ah. His infectious smile had me smiling, too.

I forgot about feeling uncomfortable around all these people. There was just Kelly and me. The song ended, and he dipped me low. This caused the applause to increase in volume. I looked into his soft brown eyes and my pulse quickened.

As he returned me to an upright position, his lips brushed the hollow of my throat. My heart skipped a beat.

I felt flustered as we made our way back to our group. Fang grinned at me. "I didn't know you were such a pretty dancer, Miss Sable."

"It was all Kelly, really," I protested. My throat tightened a little when I said his name.

"Whatever, it was still really awesome." Ophelia half hugged me in excitement. It seemed like Brandon's eyes burned a hole right through me, his posture tense and his jaw tight. A scowl turned down the corners of his mouth. Shaw left the group during the dance routines and now returned with Agent Casper on his heels. The warm fuzzy feelings from Kelly and the dismayed ones Brandon caused melded into an unsettling discomfort in my chest, which Agent Casper's presence exacerbated.

"The President is about to make his entrance. Please follow me this way." His tone was brisk and left no room for questions. We followed him as he wove through the other party goers. As an unseen announcer introduced the President and the First Lady, he ushered us through a side door.

We crowded into the room, squishing against each other to fit. I thought we resembled a very fancy looking can of sardines. Agent Casper wormed between Brandon and Chloe to stand in front of us with another man, which I assumed was his superior.

He confirmed as much as he stepped behind the unknown man. He stood a few inches shorter than Agent Casper. His hair was white blond and swirled onto the top of his head—probably an attempt to mask his receding hair line. Tension lines branched from his mouth and his eyes. Those eyes were almost black, like Fang's good eye, but lacked the warmth.

This man made it known in everything from his dress to his posture that he meant nothing but business. I tried swallowing the lump that suddenly formed in my throat, but it stuck.

"These are the Diseased from your report?" the shorter man asked.

"Yes, sir."

"Very well then. My name is Agent Hughes. I'm here to inform you that you will be exhibiting your…unique abilities…to the guests this evening. There will be nothing dangerous in nature or you will be immediately arrested by the CIA and dealt with according to the severity of your infraction. Do

I make myself clear?" He spoke in a militaristic manner, the edge in his voice cold and sharp as steel. I got the feeling he didn't take too kindly to our kind. Big surprise.

"Just to make sure we're all clear, you've invited us to this event as a form of entertainment?" Shaw uttered the last word like a curse word. His eyebrows shot up to his hairline as his hands fisted at his sides.

"Not entertainment, per se. More like an exhibition of your...talents." Agent Hughes's discomfort with referring to us as an equal species was apparent in the tick of the muscle beneath his right eye.

"Ladies and gentlemen, we now have a unique presentation for you. One of our fine CIA agents has procured a few members of the Diseased community to demonstrate their capabilities." The voice who announced the President's entrance sounded through the room we'd previously been in. The sounds of people gasping and murmuring to one another reverberated through the space.

"That's your debut," Agent Casper informed us as he pushed past us and opened the door. Fury bubbled up in my chest as we followed him out. From the looks on my companions' faces, they didn't agree with this, either.

Agent Casper stood behind a podium which appeared in our absence. He tapped the top of the microphone to ensure it worked. Thumping sounds echoed through the unseen speakers, so he glanced down at a set of note cards on the podium and began the exploitation of the freaks.

"There are seven types of Diseased standing before you: fire user, water user, electricity user, telekinetic user, kinetic energy user, soul seer, and future seer, The latter are unable to demonstrate their illnesses to you..."

I stopped listening after that. My eyes slid over to Brandon. His muscles tensed. His eyes narrowed and grew harder with every word Agent Casper spoke. The tension thickened the air in the room, making it more uncomfortable. I scanned the room for the President and the First Lady. They weren't there.

My mind raced to figure out what was happening. My train of thought was broken as a sharp pain lanced through my spine. Someone had hit me with a billy club. I stumbled forward and threw an acidic glare behind me.

"The fire user: Sable Mosley, aged sixteen. Performs well with weapons, not so well without them. Now the subject will demonstrate her fire use." Agent Casper looked at me, expectantly.

To avoid being hit again, I complied. My hands shook as I created a ball of flames in my hands.

Murmurs broke out across the room.

Satisfied with the crowd's reaction, he continued to speak. "I'll start the bidding at ten thousand dollars."

"Excuse me?" My heart stopped. My muscles were as taut as an over tightened guitar string and my mouth went dry. The flame in my hands vanished as I stood frozen in horror. I was up for auction.

Everything became a blur around me as people started shouting out numbers. The contents of my stomach roiled. I didn't realize I moved until my knees and palms hit the floor. Each number shouted served as nails driving into my ears.

My pulse pounded, causing my head to throb. Dark spots winked over my vision, reminding me to breathe.

A pair of hands seized me as chaos erupted around me. As I was yanked to a standing position, I saw a gun floating in front of Agent Casper's face. Kelly's eyes blazed as he focused on the pistol.

"Nobody move, or we'll blow a hole in his face!" Chloe growled. The crowd screamed and ran about in a panicked frenzy. Relief washed over me as Fang cradled me in his arms, but my chest was still tight.

"We'll have you arrested. Put the gun down." Agent Hughes's voice was calm, like he assumed the threat would scare us into submission. The gun turned to point at him instead. His eyes grew wide as a strangled choking noise sounded in his throat.

"You'll let us go now without a word or a fight," Shaw demanded. Agent Hughes nodded, careful not to make any sudden movements. Kelly kept his eyes trained on the gun until we made it to the entrance. It dropped to the floor as we fled.

Unfortunately, the red carpet no longer gave us a clear path out. Brandon and Shaw both cursed, using different expletives. We decided to go to the left path first, then double back if that led in the wrong direction.

The wrong direction cost us.

It was naïve to think we would make it out of this unscathed. A contingent of agents waited for us at the dead end. Chloe, Ophelia, and I had already ditched our heels, but it still proved difficult to run in ball gowns. The men never abandoned us, though. In this scenario, even they couldn't get away.

A tear slid down my cheek as I realized I was going to be a prisoner again. Flashbacks of being in Doctor Pantiel's experiment lab caused me to panic. I started hyperventilating as some of the agents produced handcuffs.

Brandon lashed out. Electricity coursed through him. He channeled that energy and directed it to the Tasers each of the agents carried. I watched in horror as they writhed on the ground. How had my life come to this? Was I always going to be on the run from people who wanted to use me? I didn't have any time to ponder over these thoughts. Brandon grabbed ahold of my wrist and dragged me after him. Adrenaline mixed with his training, and I ran as fast and as hard as I could. I made a mental note to thank him, later, for making me run all those laps.

"Which way is out?" Kelly called from behind us. Shaw and Fang ran ahead of us.

"Who cares? Just pick a door!" Brandon snarled. Shaw took his advice, and the door led out onto the back lawn. Footsteps thudded close behind us. Part of me was thankful the task force wasn't severely injured, but the other part of me cursed that they recovered so quick.

A gunshot sounded and Chloe screamed. "Kelly!"

"Keep running, damn it!" Kelly cried. I whipped my head around, finding him lying on the ground. The bullet struck him in the back of his left thigh. His face leeched of color.

"We have to go get him!" I demanded. A shadow crossed over Brandon's eyes, but he kept running. His grip on my wrist tightened. "What are you doing? We have to get him. He can't stand on his own!"

"We'll come back for him!" Shaw yelled over his shoulder. Fang doubled back to shake Chloe out of her stupor. She wouldn't budge, so he threw her over his shoulder. That seemed to jar her awake, and she screamed the whole way back to the *Kandis Amelia*.

By the time we pulled out of the harbor, I slumped onto the deck. My body was wracked with sobs. How were we supposed to go back and get Kelly? There was no way for us to tell where they'd take him. As far as I was concerned, he was as good as dead.

Shaw, Brandon, and Fang immediately started planning how to go back for him. Ophelia's eyes went blank like they did when she scanned the future. I hoped she'd find a way to get to Kelly. Chloe sat down next to me. Tears stained her cheeks, but she wasn't crying now.

"It's all your fault he got captured." Her voice was even, but acid dripped from every word.

"How?" It was all I could bring myself to say.

She crossed her arms over her chest and glowered at me. "Everyone's so concerned about you and what's happening to you and you're so oblivious to it all."

"I didn't do anything." My voice had a hollow quality.

"How can you be so blind? Brandon can't stop thinking about you. He's focused on you all the time. And Kelly—" Her voice faltered at the mention of his name. "He thinks the world revolves around you. You string them both along, pretending like you don't know they'd both do anything for you. Now Kelly has to pay the price for you. He should've let Agent Casper sell you!"

"What, and sell you next? I didn't ask for them to pay attention to me. It's horrible that Kelly got caught, but what was I supposed to do? I told Brandon to help him. Shaw said to keep running." I didn't agree with Brandon following that particular order, but he didn't ever say no to Shaw.

"It should've been you," Chloe muttered as she rose to her feet. After she was out of sight, the realization dawned on me. Even if she didn't care for me for other reasons, her acidic words were filled with so much hatred because she was jealous. She wanted Brandon to acknowledge her. Kelly...she was in love with him.

I let the thought sink deep into my brain. No wonder she'd reacted with such violence. If it was Brandon, I would behave the same way. Another realization: I'd been stringing Kelly along. Not on purpose, but that didn't make me feel any better.

I decided I had to find him. There was no other option. I just prayed Ophelia could see him. I lay down on the deck and stared up at the stars. The last thing I remembered seeing was the sun break over the horizon.

XIII

My muscles screamed in protest as I sat up. The sun was high overhead. Seagulls cawing in the distance and the scent of sea water filtered through my sleepy haze. My red silk dress had many wrinkles in it, a reminder of the struggle the night before. In a too quick flash, the memory of my almost being auctioned off like cattle and Kelly's capture assaulted my conscious mind. My tight eyes and raw throat resulted from my sobs during the night. I went to run my fingers through my hair, but it was still fastened together with the pearl tipped pins.

I groaned and sighed as I stood, trying to slow the stretching process down by using sloth-like speed to stand. The heel of my hand rubbed the remaining sleep out of my eyes. I took in a quick survey of my surroundings and found Brandon standing in front of the ship's railing a short distance away from me.

Against my better judgment, I went and stood next to him.

His normally tousled hair looked in exceptional disarray. Tension lines branched from the corners of his bloodshot eyes. A burning cigarette hung from his lips, but he wasn't inhaling it. The paper burned down, leaving a longer column of ash behind.

We both remained silent and stared out at the waves. They lapped at the side of the boat in a lazy way, then slithered back out to the ocean. The scene seemed too peaceful for the tumultuous feelings churning inside me.

"How's Chloe?" My voice sounded like someone scraped my vocal cords with sandpaper.

"Chloe?" he echoed. From the corner of my eye, I saw him turn his face toward me. Almost like he'd forgotten about it and suddenly realized it was still there, he threw his cigarette into the ocean with a jerky movement. "Damn, you look like hell."

"Thanks," I said dryly. "She seemed pretty shaken up about Kelly last night."

"Weren't we all—Did you sleep out here all night?"

"All morning. I was awake all night."

"Why'd you stay out here?"

I cast my eyes down and stared at the rusted guard railing. "It seemed too claustrophobic to go inside. Turns out the air is pretty oppressive out here, too."

"If there wasn't a difference anyhow, you should've just gone to bed."

I glanced sideways at him. He wore loose black track pants, the pair of black skate sneakers he usually wore, and no shirt.

How I missed that he wasn't wearing a shirt before, I didn't know. Faint lines traced the subtle cut of his abdominal and pectoral muscles. A slender trail of fine black hair started below his navel and disappeared beneath the waist of his pants. His broad shoulders had a rigid set to them.

He took my breath away. My teeth bit into my bottom lip, opposite my piercing. Being exposed to the salty sea air all night left them slightly chapped. "I'm going to go find Ophelia."

I stopped just before I made it to the door that led below deck. Acting on impulse, I glanced over my shoulder. Brandon's gaze met mine for only an instant, and then his head snapped back toward the vast expanse of ocean. I took the opportunity for my eyes to linger on him for a few more moments. His posture was still rigid, making the muscles in his back tense and more defined. I sighed, although I wasn't sure why, and headed down to my room.

Ophelia wasn't there when I arrived. She was most likely in Shaw's office, trying to find Kelly. I hoped Fang was with her. She'd need someone to be in her corner if she was having trouble. Chloe certainly wouldn't be.

I decided to take a shower before attempting sleep again. Upon seeing my reflection, I instantly wished I hadn't looked in the mirror. As I suspected, my hair was a tangled up mess. It was frizzy and stood on end. A few tears were evident in my dress, but didn't reveal any private areas, thank God. My mascara and eyeliner formed smudged blotches under my eyes, making the bags beneath them worse. I wrinkled my nose in disgust and then turned on the water.

It took almost ten minutes to pull all the pins out of my hair. Thankfully, the water was still warm when I finally made it into the shower.

I combed through my hair as gently as I could so it wouldn't break. After the painstaking process of untangling my hair and getting cleaned up was complete, I threw on a gray cotton spaghetti strapped shirt and a pair of black cotton briefs and flopped into bed.

As I fell asleep, visions of Brandon on the ship's deck faded in and out behind my eyelids. He appeared in my dreams, too. But my dreams showed flashes of the horrors of the nights before.

I'd been sold for fifteen thousand dollars to a scientist who reminded me of Dr. Frankenstein. As his assistants dragged me away, I screamed for Brandon. He tried to reach for me, but he'd been restrained. The rest of my companions were bound, too, and watched helplessly as I got dragged farther and farther away. The scientist spoke kindly to me while he conducted his experiments on me.

Somehow this scientist's phony niceness felt like more of a betrayal as I suffered through the agonizing torturous "experiments."

The sound of knocking at the door wrenched me from sleep. A scream escaped from me while my eyelids flew open. Brandon burst through the door, looking like he was ready for a fight. He scanned the room for a threat and then stopped cold when his eyes settled on me. Like his body was responding in slow motion, his shoulders sagged and his arms dropped to his sides.

His eyes widened, then immediately pinned themselves to the floor. A blush surfaced on his cheeks. His hand raked through the back of his hair.

My brow puckered in confusion. Surely I looked a little more presentable than when he saw me this morning. I looked down at myself to see what caused his reaction.

My eyes grew wide in horror as it dawned on me that I was half naked. I'd kicked off my blankets during my nightmare. Without grace, I scrambled to cover myself up. My skin felt hot all over, but my cheeks and ears particularly burned.

"It's just…I didn't mean…You were sleeping…What I mean is…I heard you scream and…I'm sorry," he stammered.

"It's fine, really." My voice was so quiet my words hardly reached my own ears.

"We think Ophelia might have found Kelly." He still tripped over his words a little, but his composure returned steadily.

"I'll be in Shaw's office in ten minutes." I'd managed a bit more vibrato this time.

"Right. I um…Well, that is…I'll just go tell Shaw you're on your way."

I sat in bed for a minute after he left. Apparently, dying of embarrassment was a myth. Surely that level of mortification should have killed me. When I was certain he wasn't coming back in, I hopped out of bed and went to the closet. I threw on my black zip up hoodie over my shirt and pulled on a pair of dark washed flare cut jeans.

I combed out my hair until it fell in waves. Some of the shorter pieces that used to be bangs once fell into my eyes. Normally, I would've pushed them away, but I wanted to be as covered as I could right then.

My muscles screamed in protest as I jogged to Shaw's office. They didn't hurt anything like after I'd first started training with Brandon, but it was still obnoxious. Everyone else was waiting in Shaw's office as I slipped through the door. Confusion lit Shaw's eyes as he looked me over.

"You're not wearing any shoes, but you're wearing a sweater?"

In my haste, I forgot to slip on some flip flops. I shrugged. He didn't ask me any more questions.

"So Ophelia found Kelly?" I asked.

"Not exactly," Ophelia mumbled.

"She's found someone who can help us. His name is Gareth Ramsey. He has the ability to sense someone's current location if they've been there for a certain amount of time," Shaw explained.

"Where do we find this Gareth?" Chloe asked. Her arms were folded across her chest. Her eyes were puffy and ringed with red as if she'd been crying recently.

"Somewhere in Mississippi. I think it's somewhere around Biloxi." Ophelia rubbed her temples with her index and middle fingers moving in small slow circles. A thermos sat next to her on Shaw's desk. I guessed it had coffee in it. It seemed like I wasn't the only one who was awake all night. Fang sat nearby her, a pensive expression on his face.

"So when do we go to Biloxi?" Brandon asked.

"We'll head out in the morning," Shaw decided. "I think we all deserve a good night's rest."

Everyone murmured their approval of the plan before disbanding. Fang and Ophelia headed back to their rooms. Chloe and Brandon walked off towards the training room. Shaw sat down behind his desk and unrolled a large map of the U.S. I took my leave and found myself wandering back up to the ship's deck.

The sun was almost finished setting as I stepped into the outdoors. I sat down cross-legged at the bow of the ship. The air was chilly without the sun's warmth. It made me wish I'd taken the time to put on shoes. I pulled my knees up to my chest, wrapped my arms around my legs, and rested my chin on top of my knees.

The water's lazy demeanor from the morning remained. I stared out at the vast expanse of sea before me. No matter which way I turned, no land was visible. Faint starlight began making pinpricks of white in the purple and orange hues of twilight sky.

The sound of footsteps rose to my ears, but I ignored them. I was more than happy to let my mind wander into noth-ingness. Lyrics from some of my favorite songs played in my head. Some of them made me feel better while others simulta-neously made me feel worse.

That was the thing about music: it could lift you higher, making your spirit light, or it could help you drown. I tried to hold onto the lighter lines, but the heavy ones anchored them-selves in my brain, making a dark mood churn inside me.

Whoever approached now sat next to me. I was only vaguely aware of the person to my right. My mind was still consumed with the music no one else heard.

"What are you humming?" Brandon asked.

Of course it was Brandon. And of course I didn't realize I was humming aloud. Thankfully, the darkness concealed the blush that rose to my cheeks.

"'Darkness' by Disturbed."

"I don't know that one."

"It wasn't on the radio or anything."

"Oh."

I allowed my gaze to shift from the now dark water to him. He still wore his baggy jeans like always, but he'd thrown on a black hoodie with a skateboard company's logo on the back. His eyes flicked from me to the water and back. I rested my cheek on my knees and turned my face to look at him.

He cleared his throat. "Look, I just wanted to tell you I was sorry about barging in on you earlier. I wasn't—"

I held my hand up to stop him from speaking. "I know. It's cool."

He offered a stiff nod then looked out at the water again. His legs were fully extended. He leaned back, bracing himself on his forearms so he wasn't lying flat. Then he craned his neck back so he looked at the stars. I decided to lie down, too.

One hand lay on top of the other, creating a cushion for my head to rest on. I crossed my ankles left over right.

The twilight sky was gone, leaving a glittering black curtain above us. The moon was in its new phase, leaving a black hole where it usually hung. Crashing waves created a rhythmic music, steady and calming. Despite the serene atmosphere, my heart beat a little faster than normal. Brandon had that effect on me.

"Have you ever been to Biloxi?" I asked.

"No. I heard there's lots of casinos there. Too bad I'm not old enough to get into one. I'd probably do pretty well on the poker tables." He lay down in a similar position as I was when he spoke. His hands were behind his head, too, but his legs didn't touch one another.

"Couldn't you just punch someone and get in?"

"Then I'd just get thrown out. Violence doesn't solve everything, you know."

"You could've fooled me."

His full attention was on me now. "You really think I'm that violent?" He studied me, searching for some sort of confirmation to his question.

"I think your ability to kick someone's ass is pretty compelling. Then throw in the electricity thing and that's a pretty intimidating situation."

"Are you intimidated?" His voice was soft, the crashing of the waves almost swallowing his words.

I thought about the times I'd seen him in combat or when he trained me. He was a ferocious warrior, no doubt about it. When he was in that mode, I most definitely was intimidated. But that didn't seem to be the right answer. There was something else layered in that question, something else he was asking that had nothing to do with his combat skills.

"Should I be?"

"That depends I guess." He moved closer to me, but kept a fair bit of distance between us. An electrifying energy that had nothing to do with his supernatural ability crackled between us.

Suddenly, I didn't want any distance between us at all. My hand twitched beneath my head. Acting on impulse, I sat up and spun around so I could look directly into his eyes. Despite their frosty color, they were inviting. Something lurked deep within them that I couldn't put my finger on. I moved my hand to brush the hair out of my face, but he caught it in his own.

Even though he didn't physically pull me, I felt drawn to him. Before I realized what was happening, my lips were on his. He squeezed my hand as his body went rigid, then he melted into me.

His fingers trailed up and down my spine while I deepened the kiss, my hands firmly planted on his chest. His fingers latched onto the back of my neck. My lips left his as I traced his jaw up to his earlobe with feather light kisses. The muscles in his back jolted with small spasms with each brush of my lips.

"Do you get all the new female recruits to stay this way?" I whispered in his ear.

"Never," he groaned as he unzipped my sweater a third of the way. His thumb swept over my collar bone as he pressed his lips to the hollow of my throat. Then he put his hand on my cheek. He tilted my head until our gazes locked. "There's something unique about you."

"It's the tattoo, isn't it?" I teased. "Guys dig chicks with tats."

He grinned and shook his head. "I don't know how to explain it. I'm good with my hands, not so much with my words.

But there's something about you that made me notice. Made me keep noticing. It's distracting."

"Oh." The hurt in that word threw me off.

"No, not like that! Like I said, I suck at words. It's good distracting. I want it all to myself. But I've seen that thing you have distract other people, too." At the mention of other people, his mood turned a little dark.

I had to get his focus off of whatever that dark thought was. "You're distracting, too, you know. I know how that feels, to want that distraction all to myself."

His expression softened. I linked our fingers together and he pressed a kiss on the back of my hand. I lay down next to him, my body turned toward his and my head on his chest. My eyes closed as I contented myself with listening to the sound of his steady breathing and his slightly rapid heartbeat. The scent of lemongrass and anise on his skin made me warm inside.

"Can we stay here for a while?" I asked dreamily.

"Yeah." He leaned his head down so his chin rested atop my head. Our joined hands settled next to my face. The soft rising and falling of his chest was the last thing I remembered before sleep claimed me.

XIV

"Brandon!"

The horrified shriek came from Chloe. My eyes popped open, but I couldn't make myself move away from him. He was snoring softly. His arm was thrown over his eyes like a makeshift sleep mask. He looked more boyish when he slept. I found it incredibly endearing.

"Brandon, we have company."

He twitched at my whispered words. Chloe's method of waking him up was more aggressive. I barely had time to move out of the way as her fist connected hard with his stomach. He shot to his feet, gasping and clutching at his stomach. I put my hand over my mouth in shock. He fixed a glare on Chloe.

"What the hell was that for?" he growled.

"Everyone else is waiting to have breakfast. Shaw asks me if you're ill. I go to your room to check on you. You're missing. I have a panic attack and go frantically searching for you. Then I find you having a slumber party up here with *her*." During her rant, her hands fastened to her hips. She spit the word "her" out like she wanted to use a more colorful word to describe me.

"Look, I'm sorry I freaked you out, but I can do whatever I want with whoever I choose to do it with. I'll be down in a few minutes to make breakfast. Pancakes and bacon are quick, so you can tell everyone to rest easy and that I'm just fine."

He towered over her, imposing his authority on her. She stared up at him in defiance, her mouth set in a tight line. She clutched her hips so tight her knuckles turned white.

"Fine," she said through gritted teeth. She threw a menacing glare at me as I rose to my feet. Then she stomped away, her red hair swaying back and forth like an angry flame.

When she was out of sight, I sighed. My eyes stayed glued to the deck. "I didn't mean to get you in trouble."

"Ignore her." He stretched the muscles in his back and then he twisted back and forth at his waist until his spine popped. Once he was satisfied his back was properly stretched, he held his hand out to me. I took it, and he led me below deck.

I let go of his hand begrudgingly as I took off for my room. "I guess I'll see you at breakfast."

"What's your favorite fruit?"

"What?"

"Your favorite fruit. What is it?"

I frowned in confusion. "Raspberries."

"Raspberries, huh?" He grinned as he turned to leave.

I wondered what the relevance of my favorite fruit was, but shrugged it off. The technical aspects of Brandon's cooking prowess eluded me, but I knew I liked eating whatever he made.

I changed out of my slept-in clothes into a black pleated mini skirt with ivory lace trimmed leggings and a white lace three-quarter-sleeved shirt with roses patterned into the lace with an ivory camisole beneath it. I made sure I had shoes this time, choosing teal pumps for a pop of color. I smudged black eyeliner on and applied clear gloss to my lips. I combed through my hair and wet it down, then put mousse in it and scrunched it to make tight waves in my hair. All the way to the dining room, I kept scrunching my hair to make sure it was evenly textured.

Everyone else was seated and eating, except Fang, who waited for me to start eating before he did. Brandon had managed to whip up something gourmet in the brief period it took me to make myself presentable. Apple wood smoked bacon accompanied petit sized pancakes adorned with toasted hazelnuts and a drizzle of raspberry sauce. The pancakes were fluffy and light with a touch of vanilla. Coffee and milk were served with breakfast. I opted for the milk. I wasn't much of a coffee drinker unless I couldn't taste it. I liked the smell of it, though.

Shaw announced that the trip to Biloxi would take two days. We were supposed to continue training like any other day. In Kelly's absence, Chloe got assigned to train me. She made an unpleasant snorting noise at the directive. Nausea rolled through my stomach. We agreed that her training me wasn't ideal, but Shaw stood firm on the mandate.

Fang kept a wary eye on me while we trained. Brandon and Ophelia were wholly invested in their training. I found my gaze drifting over to him while Chloe explained different maneuvers and techniques to cause as much damage as I could with the least amount of hits.

"You could at least pretend to be listening instead of making goo-goo eyes at my brother," she snapped.

"Sorry." I mumbled.

She made an exasperated sort of growl and threw her hands up in the air. "Honestly, I don't get what he sees in you. You're a weak little moron who could care less who she gets in trouble. You only care about yourself. You don't give a damn about who you hurt as long as you get your way." Her eyes bored into mine while she spoke, each word dripping with more acid than the last.

"You're one to talk about being weak. You're sloppy and you can't even manipulate water unless it's in a pretty little bowl right in front of you."

Her eyes grew wide and her mouth fell open. After her tirade about my lack of awareness of others, I wasn't feeling too charitable.

"You just like everyone paying attention to you. You like how Fang looks out for you like family and Ophelia's there for your moral support. Then you've got Brandon and Kelly both falling all over themselves to get your attention. And Shaw thinks you're something special because you can light yourself on fire without killing yourself.

"I'll bet after we find this Gareth guy that you'll expect him to go crazy over you like everyone else. Well, I have news for you. You're not worth any of their time. You're especially not worth my time. You can train yourself and have another reason for everyone to think you're awesome, even though you're nothing more than a spoiled, egocentric waste."

Everyone watched as she stormed out of the room, the door clanging shut behind her.

I stood in place, too awestruck to do anything else. No one else moved, either. I stared at the wall ahead of me without my eyes really focusing on anything. Without meaning to, I slumped against the wall and slid to the floor.

"Miss Sable…" Somewhere in my fuzzy vision, Fang appeared. Every sound that reached my ears was distorted by the static buzzing in my brain. Where had that come from? I knew Chloe wasn't too crazy about me to begin with, and I knew she was upset because she had feelings for Kelly but he seemed to be interested in me. Could that really have provoked such animosity?

"I just…I need a minute, okay?" I stood on shaky legs and moved slowly to the door. I felt three pairs of eyes on me as I let the door click shut.

I spent the next day and a half with my head kept low. At meals, I ate quickly and went back to my room. Ophelia and Fang tried to make small talk with me, but I couldn't bring myself to engage. I avoided Brandon at all costs.

Finally, Shaw announced we'd arrived in Mississippi. Everyone had something else to focus on: find Gareth Ramsey and rescue Kelly. Shaw rented a conversion van under a false name once we were on shore. Fang, who'd become Shaw's protégé, sat up front with him.

Chloe and Brandon sat in the captain's chairs behind them, leaving the bench seat that turned into a bed for Ophelia and me. Shaw also procured a tourist map of all the casinos in the area since Ophelia's vision showed us finding Gareth at a craps table.

The air was thick and hot and humid, even with the air conditioner running. Even though I wasn't moving, I was sweating. I'd knotted my hair on top of my head, but loose strands of it stuck to my neck and my face.

Despite the sticky air around us, the scenery was picturesque. Little tourist shops dotted the road across from the beach. White sand sprawled across the shore, some darkened from the tide rolling in over it. Palm trees swayed to and fro in the breeze. Seagulls cawed to one another and scoured the beach for leftovers from tourist cook outs.

Visually, the only flaw was the shells of grand houses that remained after the rest of the homes were washed away by torrential hurricanes.

Since we were too young to walk on the casino floors, Brandon, Chloe, and I were instructed to stay in the van while Shaw, Fang, and Ophelia scoured the casinos for Gareth. It took ten hours to comb through six casinos to come up empty handed.

"Shaw, maybe everyone should get some rest and then you guys can keep looking tomorrow," I suggested.

"We'll search one more, and then we'll call it a night." Shaw turned into the parking lot of the Treasure Bay Casino and Hotel. The structure wasn't very impressive. A modest brown and beige building with the casino's name scrawled across the top of it. Behind it was a building that reminded me of an office. It was long instead of tall, although it was a few stories high. I could tell by the backlit blue drapes in the windows that those were the hotel rooms.

The three eldest got out of the van, leaving the youngest of us behind again. Brandon worked on sharpening a dagger he brought with him.

Chloe attempted to sleep in the captain's chair she'd sat in all day. I folded the bench seat down to make the mattress and lay down on it. I stared at the roof of the van and folded my hands over my abdomen.

The grain in the wood paneling on the roof started blurring together when I felt Brandon climb onto the bench seat/mattress next to me.

"Brandon—"

"She's just jealous, you know. And she's used to being the center of attention with me. It's just been us since we were kids. She's always been my number one. But she sees how I am with you and she's freaked out that I'm replacing her. I told her that would never happen, but the chip is still on her shoulder." He smiled at me and kissed my cheek. "She'll come around."

Footsteps sounded outside the van. The jingle of keys put us all on alert. Chloe snapped awake and searched for silhouettes outside the van windows, just like we did at the other six casinos. I expected to see three figures outside the van. My heart skipped a couple of beats when I saw four.

The doors opened and Gareth crawled in behind Ophelia. He was tall like Brandon and Kelly, with the same lean muscular build.

His light brown hair was styled in a faux hawk. Deep sapphire blue eyes surveyed us as Fang made him sit in the back seat with Brandon and me.

He wore a navy, long-sleeved shirt with a white T-shirt over it that said in black letters, *If I sneeze around you, it's because I'm allergic to stupid people.*

Tan workman's boots peeked out from under the hem of his dark, washed, boot-cut jeans. His square jaw was set in a pensive frown.

An uncomfortable silence permeated through the van as we drove back to the ship. Gareth sat between Brandon and me. Brandon palmed his dagger: a sign that if Gareth thought about moving an inch without permission, Brandon could deal quite a bit of damage. I felt bad for Gareth. It was almost like we were treating him as a prisoner instead of someone whose help we needed.

Shaw dropped the rest of us off at the *Kandis Amelia* with instructions to wait for his return in his office. He planned to catch a cab back from the car rental lot. Everyone kept a wary eye on each other. Gareth sat in the middle of us all, clearly making silent mental notes about each of us in turn. Chloe and Brandon stood in front of him while Fang, Ophelia, and I stood behind him.

My body started to feel how late it was and the terrible sleep I'd gotten the last few nights. My muscles and joints were stiff and groaned in protest when I stretched my arms over my head and yawned.

Fang smiled at me. "Miss Sable, surely you can get some rest. We can watch over Mr. Ramsey until Shaw gets back,"

I was about to take him up on it when Chloe interjected.

"Shaw told us all to be here, so she stays." Her hazel eyes narrowed into a steely glare.

A chill ran up my spine. My eyes couldn't stay focused on hers.

"Really, ah, Sable was it? Don't worry about what the rocko says. You don't have to have five people watching one person." Gareth spoke with a British accent. He glanced over his shoulder get a better look at me.

I blinked. "The rocko?"

"That one with the bright red hair there. She thinks she's intimidating but she looks like a pixie. I'd be more inclined to take orders from your friend here." The latter statement indicated Fang.

"Look British boy—" Chloe snarled.

"Welsh, actually," Gareth interrupted.

"No one cares. You're here on a mission. I don't know by what means Shaw 'convinced you to come here,' but you're not likely to gain anything by insulting us." She clasped her hands on her hips and sneered while she ranted.

"And you think you're going to get me to find your missing boyo if you make hollow threats like that?" He crossed his arms over his chest and sunk back in his chair. Chloe's cheeks turned scarlet. "The fact is, miss, that you need my skills. I don't have to be here."

"Right. And despite my colleague's horrible manners, we're very thankful you're willing to help us," Ophelia soothed. She shot a dark look at Chloe, whose color turned

from scarlet to purple. Her hands fisted at her sides and a muscle ticked in her jaw.

Gareth swiveled his chair around so he faced Ophelia,
Fang, and me. His eyes studied Ophelia's. "You're the girl
who found me in the casino."

"Yes. My name is Ophelia. This is Fang, and this is Sable.
The boy behind you is Brandon, and his ill-tempered sister,
Chloe." She indicated each of us with her index finger, point-
ing at each of us in turn.

A smirk played on Gareth's thin lips. "I guess it's true
what they say about red heads then, eh?"

Brandon hastily covered a chuckle with a cough when
Chloe cast her murderous glare on him.

Before Chloe could make a retort, Shaw strode into his
office. Without noticing the tension in the room, he sat behind
his desk and folded his hands atop it. Heavy bags hung under
his eyes, a product of his lack of sleep.

"Mr. Ramsey, thank you for agreeing to help us in our
time of need. As I explained to you in the casino, one of our
own was captured and we don't know where to find him.

"I'll offer you lodging, food, and whatever other necessi-
ties you require while your services are being rendered. Do
you agree to the terms?" Shaw extended his hand to Gareth,
who shook it after a moment's pause.

"I'll need one of his possessions," Gareth informed us.

"We'll provide one for you tomorrow. For now, I think
it's best if we all get a decent night's sleep. Brandon will show
you to your room. Notify him or Chloe if there's anything else
you require."

Gareth looked at Brandon and grinned. "I don't think I'll
bother with that lot, seeing as she's not too keen on me. Looks
like we're going to be mates, bro."

Chloe stomped out of the room before the rest of us starting milling toward the door.

Brandon caught my hand in his and squeezed it before escorting Gareth to his room.

It turned out that he'd be staying two doors down from Ophelia and me.

As I changed into my pajamas, I noticed Ophelia almost fluttering about. I sat on the edge of my bed and gave her one of those looks that told her I knew something was up.

She caught my stare and settled in front of me on the edge of her bed.

"Okay, spill," I demanded.

"He's gorgeous, isn't he?" she gushed.

"Gareth?"

"Yes, Gareth! Who else?"

"Uh, sure. His accent is sexy."

"I know, right?"

It was true that I found his accent attractive. That was about the extent of it, though. It wasn't that he wasn't good looking, because he was.

Brandon consumed all my thoughts about cute boys, so I had a bias.

"We should probably get some sleep." I lay down on my bed and snuggled up beneath the blankets. "He might need some defending if Chloe's going to keep acting like that toward him."

"If she keeps giving you that attitude, I think she'll need some defending, too," she remarked as she turned off the lamp on the bedside table.

"Well, you can help out Gareth, and Fang can protect me." I laughed. "Honestly, though, I don't know if anyone can protect me against the wrath of Chloe,"

"That's true. We'll figure something out. Goodnight, Sable."

"Goodnight Ophelia."

XV

When I woke up the next morning, Ophelia wasn't there. I guessed she was already up and ready to make an impression on Gareth. No doubt everyone else was at breakfast, but I didn't feel like eating anything.

The solitude of the ship's deck was calling to me. I dressed in a pair of form-fitting, red jeans with black accents on the pockets and billowy black halter top with black wedge flip flops. My hair was fastened at the nape of my neck in a loose pony tail.

The weather was pleasant outside. It wasn't humid like it was in the heat of the day in the South. A light breeze made the palm trees sway listlessly. The sun shone brightly, making the water of the Gulf glitter.

A few tourists, looking to stake out the best tanning spots, wandered on the beach. Some men stood on the dock, fishing poles in hand. Seagulls cawed to one another overhead. The wind blew a few loose strands of my hair across my face. I let them tickle my skin. The sensation made my nose wrinkle.

Eventually, the itchy quality of the feeling made me brush the hair away.

I sat down with my legs spread apart and rested my weight on my palms behind me, soaking in the rays of sunshine, thankful for the few precious moments alone. Sooner or later, Fang or Brandon would come looking for me. Or Kelly, if he'd been there.

My light mood became heavy when I thought of him. Where was he? Did the government still have him? Did they sell him to one of those horrible scientists? That train of thought left me thankful I hadn't eaten.

Begrudgingly, I stood and made my way down to Shaw's office, where everyone would undoubtedly be waiting for Gareth to find Kelly. How specific would the location be? Chloe would probably strangle Gareth outright if he couldn't figure it out. A wisp of sympathy for the boy rose in me at that thought.

As I stepped into Shaw's office, the scene that greeted me was what I expected. Everyone sat around Gareth, who was holding an old wallet of Kelly's in his hands. His eyes looked vacant the way Ophelia's did when she glimpsed the future. They flicked back and forth at a rapid pace until he blinked. He shook his head as if he was trying to clear out a lingering vision.

"Kelly Armstrong is in Canada."

"Canada's a big place, son. Which providence is he in?" Shaw asked with a grim expression.

"Yukon."

"Where the hell is that?" Chloe demanded.

"Near Alaska," Fang answered.

Gareth rubbed his temples with his index and middle fingers in small circles. "There's a secret military base there that he's being held in."

"That's a good start, at least. Good work, Ramsey." Shaw clapped his hand on Gareth's shoulder before walking out of his office. The rest of us followed behind him and set off in different directions. Ophelia and Gareth went with Shaw, Fang headed towards the training room, and Chloe went in the direction of her room. Brandon caught my shoulder as I walked through the doorway.

"Hold on a minute," he beseeched.

I stopped walking, but I didn't turn around. "What?"

"What's up with you lately? You don't seem to be around anymore unless we're eating. Then you hardly touch your food before you run off again."

"Nothing. I'm just worried about Kelly, that's all." It was a lie, but a necessary one. I didn't expect lying to him to hurt me, but a physical pang of guilt stabbed in my chest.

"We'll find him, don't worry."

"Maybe you should go check on Chloe?" I turned just in time to see his face fall. He gave a stiff nod, released my shoulder, and followed after her.

She was the real reason I'd been avoiding him. Her angry glare burned into me, even when she wasn't around. She didn't like Brandon paying attention to me, although I didn't know why. I had a feeling, though, that her malice wasn't specifically branded to me. Any girl Brandon found interesting probably ground her gears.

In any case, I certainly didn't want to come between siblings. So I did the best to ignore the butterflies in my stomach and my fluttering heart when we were near each other. Not an easy task, but a necessary one.

I wandered down to the training room. Fang was deeply involved in his weight training regimen when I entered. At the metallic clang of the shutting door, his eyes landed on me. A broad grin stretched across his face as he took me in.

"If I might say, Miss Sable, you're looking healthier all the time."

He, Ophelia, and I all were. Six weeks had passed since our escape from the asylum. Fang's muscles bulged beneath his skin now. Ophelia's hourglass curves had filled out, giving her a sultry appearance that softened her edgy '80s throwback style. I was still slender, but my hips had gained some shape, making me look more balanced and not so much like a little boy.

"I smiled and winked at him. You don't look too bad yourself."

He chuckled and put the weights he held down while I approached him. His grin disappeared as I got closer.

"There's something troubling you." An accusation, not a question.

"After we get Kelly back, what are we supposed to do? I mean, it's great that Shaw took us in and is training us and all, but what's it all for? It'll be nice not to randomly set things on fire, but what else is there?" I paced the floor while I spoke.

His answer surprised me. "Have you ever asked Brandon or Chloe why they stayed?"

"No." I blinked. I'd never thought to. I couldn't now that Chloe hated me and I was avoiding Brandon at all costs. "Have you?"

"No. I reckon Ophelia will know when it's time to leave."

"When Brandon broke us out of the asylum, did she know he was coming?" I sat down where I stood. Fang sat down on the bench of the at home gym and started working on his deltoids.

"Yeah, she did. But she said the universe was waiting for someone else's actions to set the rescue in motion. I don't know what all that means, but you showed up, he came, and now we're here." A sheen of sweat on his dark chocolate colored skin made it glisten under the harsh fluorescent lights.

I tapped my chin with my index finger while I thought over Fang's information. Maybe I needed to have a talk with Brandon after all.

I threw my arms around Fang and kissed his cheek.

The grin returned to his face as he placed his palm atop the spot I kissed. "What was that for?"

"For being brilliant! I'll talk to you later, okay?" I was out the door before he had time to respond.

Lately, if I wanted to find Brandon, I'd usually be able to find him on the ship's deck. I ran through the corridors until I found the stairwell that led outside. My feet pounded up the metal steps, banging loudly as I went. I threw open the door and skidded to a halt to survey my surroundings. My head swiveled back and forth until I found Brandon standing at the stern of the ship. The wisp of smoke above his head indicated that a lit cigarette rested between his lips.

"Brandon!" I panted as I ran to him. I shoved my arms out in front of me and caught the guard rail in my hands with a loud thud.

He threw his cigarette into the ocean and regarded me with alarm. "What's wrong?" His eyes blazed with a mixture of panic and calculation.

"Nothing, I just wanted to talk to you," I said, still trying to catch my breath.

"Now you want to talk—"

"I know I've been all weird and crazy the past few days. I'm sorry. But I really need to talk to you."

He wore an expression of bemusement as I rambled. After a moment's pause, he nodded, telling me to continue.

I stared at him with earnest. "Why did you stay here with Shaw after he trained you? Why didn't you take Chloe to Paris and become a chef like you wanted to?"

"Where else was I supposed to go? I was a kid with no parents and no money." He flopped down onto the deck and sat cross legged. I sat next to him and drew my knees up to my chest. "Besides, I believe in Shaw's mission."

"What's Shaw's mission?"

We stared out at the water, watching people sail their boats and yachts in the distance.

"When he gets enough of us together and trained, he's going to show the world we're not just good for human shields. Our abilities are an extension of who we are, not what defines us. We're people, too. Some people are good athletes, some are good musicians, and others are good with numbers or words. They're not considered freaks for excelling in something." Passion filled his words. It was contagious.

"To be fair, I think guys using steroids to bulk up for enhanced sports performance is a little less shocking than me being able to start fires at will or you being able to electrocute someone."

He laughed at this.

"Okay, maybe you have a point. But we're still human underneath it all. Shaw wants everyone else to see that, too."

"I don't feel very human most of the time," I admitted. From the corner of my eye, I saw him turn his head and look at me. I turned my head, too, and my eyes locked with his.

"Now can I ask you something?"

I shrugged. "Fair's fair I guess."

"Why did you get those stars tattooed by your eye?"

"To piss off my parents."

He brushed the tattoo lightly with his fingertips. It sent a shiver up my spine. "You probably could've gotten any tattoo to piss them off. Why that one?"

"Maybe it was to get noticed. But I tried to be as unnoticeable as I could. Pretty contradictory I guess. I wanted my parents to notice me, not the girl who started fires. I wanted to hide from everyone else."

I turned my attention back to the Gulf then. Brandon placed his hand on my cheek and gently steered my face back to his. He sat closer to me than he had before. My breath caught, and I cursed myself inwardly for it. His gaze melted my insides. The butterflies in my stomach fluttered wildly.

"You don't need that to get noticed. They look nice and all, but your eyes stand out all on their own."

Unable to resist any longer, I laid my head on his shoulder. Then I decided to come clean about my earlier lie. "I've been avoiding you because of your sister. I don't think she likes us being together so much."

He sighed and laid his hand down on top of mine, which still clutched my knees to my chest. "Don't worry about her so much. She's overprotective, that's all."

I doubted that was all, but I didn't tell him so. "You're pretty protective of her, too."

"All we have is each other. When we first ran away from home, we promised we'd always have each other's backs. It's more than being brother and sister. It's hard to explain. She's all I've ever really cared about. Then you came along and something else took over..."

Maybe he knew more about Chloe's true feelings than I thought.

"I always wanted siblings. Fang's like my big brother, though. I'm lucky we happened to share a cell. I wouldn't have lasted in that dungeon without him." The memories of the horrors I'd endured at the Crazy Cannon Place caused me to shiver. I preferred "the being infatuated" shivers to this one.

"We were lucky that Shaw found us and not some other sadistic psycho."

"Why did you come to the asylum anyhow?"

"When Ophelia came here years ago, she told Shaw that in six years she'd be held captive there and need rescuing. That was the only prediction she made for him, and Shaw wanted to see if it was real. So he sent me to check it out. I was supposed to bring her back with me if I found her. Chloe's not great at warming up to new people, so she didn't want me to find Ophelia. That's why she was so upset when I brought all three of you. I struck gold when you insisted on getting Ophelia before we spilt."

"How does Shaw have all this money to keep this ship going and sending you out on missions and buying us clothes and food?"

Brandon hooked a lock of hair around my ear and put his arm around me. "His parents died in a house fire when he was in his thirties. They were billionaires and he was an only child. I guess they were in the oil business. Anyway, the money all went to him."

The sun burned high overhead, indicating it was just past noon. Just as my brain registered the time, my stomach growled. My cheeks burned with embarrassment. He chuckled as he released me.

"Come on, let's get you something to eat." He held his hand out to help me up and I took it. "Do you want to help me cook lunch?"

"I don't cook."

A smirk played on his lips. "What do you do, then?"

"Read. A lot. I love reading." Reading was the best escape I knew. I loved getting wrapped up in the stories and the characters' relationships.

He smiled and led me down to the kitchen. "Then you can read the recipes in the cookbook."

The kitchen was rather modest in size, but the appliances were state of the art. A four burner gas stove sat next to a double oven on the left wall. Straight ahead of me were a large refrigerator and a deep freezer. Lining the right wall were metal cabinets which, Brandon explained, held the dry goods, bowls, and other cooking utensils, and the cookbooks. The wall behind me had an industrial three basin sink and an additional sink that was used to descale and debone fish. A large island sat in the middle of the space, leaving little room to maneuver around it. Pots and pans hung from a rectangular pot rack mounted into the ceiling. Everything was chrome colored except for the top of the island, which was made of black marble. I let out a low whistle while Brandon grabbed ingredients out of the cabinets and fridge.

"What are we making?" I asked. Some of the ingredients I recognized: lobster, tomatoes, cornmeal, and cheese. The different green herbs he got from the fridge I couldn't identify. He filled a large stock pot with water and put it on the stove. The stove made a clicking noise when he turned the knobs to light the pilot light.

"Crap. I can't get it to light. Maybe the propane tanks need to be changed." He started to bend down to look beneath the stove as I tapped him lightly on the shoulder.

"May I?"

Brandon's brow puckered in confusion, but he stepped aside. I moved the pot off of the burner and found the pilot light on each burner. I concentrated on a small flame appearing on each one, and they appeared one by one, just like in my head.

"Huh. I didn't even think to use your fire power. I need to remember to put matches on the shopping list." He moved the stock pot back onto the burner and adjusted the flame. While he waited for the water to boil, he started washing and crushing tomatoes in another pot.

"What are you making?"

"We are making lobster pizza. Come here."

I walked over and stood next to him. "Where's this cookbook I'm supposed to be reading?"

"I know this recipe."

"So I'm just supposed to stand here and watch?"

"No, you're supposed to slice the basil."

My nose wrinkled as I tried to discern which of the herbs on the island was basil. He laughed, put some leafy looking herbs on the cutting board, and handed me a knife.

I took the knife from him and held it as close to the end of the handle as I could. Then I drew the blade over the leaves but didn't quite cut through them all the way.

"Here, hold the knife like this," Brandon instructed as he stood behind me and put his arms over mine. He slid my hand up closer to the blade of the knife. Then he rolled the basil leaves up into tight spirals. "Cut them diagonally. It releases more aroma and flavor that way, plus it makes nice green strips to put on top of the pizza."

The warmth of his body so close to mine made my skin tingle. I cut the basil like he told me to. The air filled with a sweet earthy scent. While I sliced the other herbs, he concocted the tomato sauce and put the lobsters into the boiling water. The lobster part was kind of disturbing. It was almost like they were screaming when they hit the water. I had a momentary consideration of adopting a vegan lifestyle.

To lighten my mood, I tried to picture him as a little boy, making pizzas with his father. The boy in my head had smudges of flour on his chin and shaggy black hair peeking out from beneath an oversized floppy chef hat. His father, an older version of the Brandon I knew, carefully corrected him when he was too hasty or careless. It was a sweet thought.

"What's so funny?" Brandon's voice jarred me from my imaginings. He'd pulled the pizza dough from the refrigerator and was rolling it out into a rectangle.

My cheeks turned bright red. "Nothing."

"Okay, time to build the pizza. Here, dust the pizza crust with corn meal. Then flip it over and we'll put the sauce and the toppings on it." I did as I was instructed. Then he swirled the tomato sauce over the dough with the back of a ladle. Next, he laid pieces of shaved mozzarella cheese over the pie, followed by a sprinkling of shredded provolone cheese. The lobster and basil and some fresh diced tomatoes topped the pizza. Before sticking it into the oven, he brushed the crust with melted butter infused with garlic.

"How long do we have to wait?"

"Patience is a virtue, you know."

"So is the use of platitudes," I replied as I wiped off the island. When I finished cleaning it, I helped Brandon wash the dirty dishes and put them away.

"Well, we still have about ten minutes until the pizza is ready," he assessed.

"Should we go tell the others that lunch is almost ready?"

"There's time for that later." We stood inches apart. Every nerve ending in my body was hyper aware of the close proximity. My fingers twitched, begging to knot themselves in his messy tresses.

"And now?" I breathed.

He wrapped his arms around me and pressed his lips to mine. My arms wound around him as I answered back with my own kisses. Then he pressed my body closer to his, the lemongrass and anise scent of him making me dizzy. In one fluid movement, he picked me up and set me down on top of the island. My legs wound around his waist and my fingers knotted in his hair while he left a hot trail of kisses down my neck. Between torrid pecks, he groaned, "Sable—"

Ding! The timer went off on the oven. Reluctantly, I let go of him with shaky hands. He still held tightly to me, his face buried between my neck and shoulder.

"Brandon, lunch…"

"Let it burn." His words were muffled by my hair.

"Brandon."

It almost ached when he finally released me.

After he opened the oven door, the scent of basil and tomato and mozzarella wafted through the air. It made my mouth water. My stomach growled again, reminding me how hungry I was. He drizzled the pizza with extra virgin olive oil before cutting it into squares and sliding it onto a serving platter.

"It looks amazing!" I gushed as we went in search of the others.

"Oh? I didn't notice." He grabbed my hand and twined our fingers together.

Chloe would just have to get over herself. Brandon consumed me, and I never wanted that to change.

XVI

The climates in Biloxi and the Yukon contrasted like night and day. Biloxi was warm and sunny and breezy. The Yukon was gray, cold, and damp. It was surprising to find just a light dusting of snow covering the ground. Then again, it was only mid-October. Despite the chill in the air, I was happy to be off the *Kandis Amelia*. All that steel made me a little depressed. I stuffed my hands into the pockets of my fur trimmed black suede winter jacket and stared out at the barren expanse in front of me.

Thick gray clouds clung desperately to the atmosphere, creating a delicate fog around us. Tree stumps littered the ground, giving the landscape a knobby looking texture. Loggers must've cleared the area since none of the wood had a charred appearance.

Gareth stood next to me with a blank expression on his face. His glassy, jewel-toned blue eyes stared unblinking ahead. Despite his slack facial features, his spine could've been made of a taught rubber band ready to snap at any moment, pulling his shoulders back, making them strained. He clutched Kelly's worn brown leather wallet in his left hand. One by one, Shaw, Fang, Ophelia, Brandon, and Chloe stood in front of Gareth and me, waiting for Gareth to snap out of his vision and give us Kelly's location. As I looked around at each member of our posse, I had a fleeting thought of what we'd look like in a comic book with coordinating uniforms to kick ass in. There's no way we'd ever agree on a design since our tastes in clothes were all vastly different.

After what seemed like hours—although I'm sure it wasn't more than twenty minutes—Gareth's eyes blinked rapidly as his conscious mind returned to his body. His shoulders sagged and he breathed out a long sigh. "Kelly's being held in a cabin about forty miles east of here. He's not hurt, for now, but we shouldn't waste time."

"Well, back to your trucks then, troops," Shaw instructed.

The first thing we did when we landed just outside of Juneau, Alaska, was rent vehicles. Since they didn't have any conversion vans or SUVs available, Shaw rented a yellow hard top Jeep Wrangler and allowed Brandon to pick out a blue Ford Shelby—after much prodding on Brandon's part.

Shaw, Gareth, Ophelia, and Fang rode in the Jeep while Brandon, Chloe, and I rode in the Shelby. Chloe sat sprawled out in the back seat and I sat up front with Brandon. He was teaching me how to tell when to switch gears in a manual transmission vehicle. My hand clasped the top of the gear shifter and his hand rested atop mine. The nerve endings in my whole arm hummed at his touch.

An hour had passed when Shaw abruptly stopped the Jeep in front of us. Brandon swerved to the left, avoiding a collision. Chloe's fingernails dug into the headrest on either side of my head. Another couple of inches in and she would've clawed my face. Everyone clambered out of their vehicles and received instructions from Gareth. We'd have to walk the rest of the way there so our rescue mission wouldn't be discovered.

The walk was on a private drive that went uphill. As I huffed it as best I could, I stared in wonderment at Chloe, who never broke stride in her stiletto boots. Since I'd been training with Brandon, the hike wasn't as tough as I'd anticipated. My calves burned when we finally reached the cabin, but if I hadn't gone through training, I wouldn't have made it up the hill.

The cabin was made of thick maple logs stacked atop each other and interlocked at the corners. A plywood door with a round brass handle screwed into it was the only interruption in the square of logs. More of the same logs made up a slanted roof. One side of the cabin must be higher than the other, I realized. There were no windows.

Shaw motioned for Brandon and Fang to come with him to the door. The rest of us stayed where we were and watched as Shaw tried the handle without making a sound. It was unlocked. A puzzled expression screwed up Brandon's profile. My stomach twisted into a tight knot. Every spy movie I'd ever seen with a rescue in it, the captive was behind a locked door. This was a trap.

As if my thoughts summoned them, almost thirty men dressed in camouflage outfits ambushed us. Brandon cursed aloud, and I think Gareth did, too, but it was some slang word that I didn't recognize. Subconsciously, we formed a tight circle with our backs to each other.

"What can we do?" Ophelia asked, her tone sounding almost resigned.

"Go down swinging," Shaw replied.

I couldn't see him, but I pictured him in my mind with his mouth set in a hard line, determination written in his features.

The men advanced on us, machine guns drawn. I focused my mind on creating a circle of flames around us. After a few moments, the crackle of burning dry leaves sounded. Some of the men jumped back in surprise. Fang, who stood to my right, grabbed my hand and squeezed it. Sweat beaded on my brow, partially from the heat of the fire and partially from the exertion of keeping it in place.

One man stepped forward and slung his gun behind his back. He held his hands up like he was surrendering, but I knew better. With some effort, I made the flames shoot up a foot to let him know I wasn't fooled by his show.

"You can't keep that wall up forever. It'd be easier if you just came with us. Besides, don't you want to see your friend?" He kept his tone even, but his smug expression said he knew he had us cornered.

"If you did anything to Kelly I'll—" Chloe started.

"Shut up, Chloe." A warning, not a request, from Brandon. Chloe didn't speak again.

"Just come with us. I assure you your comrade is completely safe and unharmed," the spokesman for the miniature militia promised.

"And what happens if we come with you?" Shaw asked.

The spokesman walked around to look Shaw in the eye when he answered. Well, as much as you could look someone in the eye when you wore a helmet that hid your whole head.

"We have a business proposition for you. Our commander will explain everything to you. We don't want to harm you, but if you don't cooperate, we will take you by force." A promise, not a threat.

After an agonizing stretch of silence, Shaw agreed that we'd go with them. Gareth mumbled something unintelligible under his breath. I started getting dizzy and my knees shook, so I extinguished the wall of flames. The crackle of electricity buzzed in the air when the fire was gone.

"Brandon, I said we'd go with them. We're not going to fight them here," Shaw said gently.

The electrically charged air disappeared, and in single file, we followed Shaw, who followed the spokesman. Brandon walked in front of me. I grabbed his hand and he linked our fingers together. Militia men flanked us on both sides, making me feel claustrophobic. I'm sure everyone else's mind spun the same questions. Why did Shaw agree to go with these men? Where were we going? Were they lying about Kelly's welfare?

It was difficult to determine where exactly we traveled with all the militia men surrounding us. After about an hour of walking, we stopped. Looming above us was a realistic looking artificial maple tree. It reminded me of cell phone towers modeled after palm trees, I saw once on a vacation with my parents in Florida. The thought of my parents caused a fleeting pang in my chest. I couldn't afford to open that can of worms just now. Brandon still held tightly onto my hand and my fingers twitched. He gave my hand a reassuring squeeze.

When I got to the tree trunk, I saw a door opened in the base of the trunk revealing a staircase. Spearheaded by the spokesman, we climbed down the stairs, followed by the militia men. It was wide enough for us to walk with two people side by side, so I walked down with Brandon. I flicked my gaze to his face a few times during our descent. It was a mask of determination and calculation, giving away no emotion. I attempted schooling my face into something similar. My nose scrunched up and my eyebrows knit together, so I abandoned trying to keep a neutral expression.

The stairwell, which was lit by gas burning lamps spread about fifteen feet apart, opened into a dimly lit square with a low ceiling. Brandon and Fang just barely avoided having to bend down to walk into the room. The floor was made of hard packed earth, as were the walls and ceiling. Gas lamps were mounted into the walls, making a glowing border around the room. At the opposite end, about twenty paces away, stood the commander of the militia, a few guards, and Kelly. Chloe inhaled sharply, but otherwise stayed silent and stood in place. Kelly regarded us all with an expression of genuine interest, like he didn't expect us to be there.

"Captain Marsh, I've found the rogue clan of Diseased that Private Anderson used to be a part of," the spokesman said.

Captain Marsh nodded. "Thank you, Marshall Greer. You may stand down."

"Yes, sir." Marshall Greer moved to join the rest of the militia men standing behind us.

Captain Marsh studied us each in turn. "Mr. Shaw, you're the leader of this little...group...are you not?"

"For your purposes, yes, I am," Shaw agreed. He stepped forward as he spoke and crossed his arms over his chest.

"Private Anderson tells me you've trained your soldiers well. Judging by his abilities, I would agree that that's true."

"What is it exactly that you want?"

Captain Marsh smirked and anchored his hands on his hips. "Since you insist, let's skip the pleasantries and get right down to business. We're with the United States government. Our liaisons in the Canadian government have allowed us to use this abandoned post for our meeting with you. We're with a special task force called the D.A.O. that works with members of the Diseased. If you come to work with us, we offer you security, anonymity, and a chance at a normal life."

"D.A.O.?" I asked.

"Diseased Affairs and Operations," he answered, without taking his sharp hazel eyes off of Shaw.

"It's really a great deal. You get your own house, a government job with all the benefits, and the best part is that you don't have to worry about being hunted down anymore," Kelly explained.

"What's to become of us when we're no longer of use to you?" Shaw asked skeptically.

I was relieved that someone besides me found this offer suspicious. Something about the way Captain Marsh carried himself made me feel uneasy. I couldn't quite put my finger on it, though.

Captain Marsh waved his hand like he was swatting away a fly. "That's semantics."

"And what if we don't want to join?" This time, it was Gareth who spoke up.

"Then we'll return you to your vehicles and you can be on your way," Captain Marsh said with a smile as sharp as a steel blade. It made a chill run up my spine.

"Thank you for your gracious offer, but we'd like to be going now," Shaw replied with forced politeness.

"Very well then."

"Wait a second. I–I want to join you," Chloe said.

Brandon's fingers ripped away from mine as he whirled around to face his sister.

"You what?"

"I'm tired of fighting and hiding. Don't you want to be normal, Brandon? Don't you want to be free and live your dream of being a chef?"

"I…"

Brandon looked like the words he tried to speak got stuck in his throat. I knew that idea would be tempting to him. It's what he'd dreamed about since he was a kid.

"Yes, you could be a chef for our organization. We would even put you through culinary school, if that's what you desire to do," Captain Marsh piped up.

"Culinary school?" Brandon's voice was soft as if his mind was far away from the present.

I couldn't shake my gut feeling that something was wrong with this proposition. Why would the government just give us all of these things? What did they want in return? And why didn't Captain Marsh answer Shaw's question about what happened to us when we weren't needed anymore?

"Brandon, don't. It's not right." I could barely hear the words coming out of my mouth.

"Brandon, come with your sister," Kelly instructed.

Brandon's hand twitched.

"Come with me Brandon," Chloe pleaded.

I didn't want Chloe to go, either, but I knew she wouldn't listen to me. Why wasn't anyone else trying to convince her to leave with us?

"It's your decision, Brandon." Shaw clapped a hand on Brandon's shoulder before he turned his attention to Chloe. The sadness in his eyes reminded me of a father letting his child go on a journey he didn't agree with. "If you really wish to leave, I hope you find what you're seeking through the D.A. O."

I moved to stand in front of Brandon while Chloe went to stand next to Kelly. "Brandon, come with me."

He stared at Chloe. The pain in his eyes spoke of a boy torn between two things he loved: his sister and his adoptive father.

I held his face in my palms and gently guided him to look into my eyes. "Something's wrong with this. Don't go."

"What will it be, young Brandon? It seems your comrades would like to leave." Captain Marsh arched a brow and crossed his arms over his chest. "Will you be going with them or staying with us?"

"Chloe...I'm sorry..." He choked on the words as he spoke them and looked at the ground.

Chloe looked like someone had punched her in the stomach. Kelly put an arm around her waist in support. Brandon ripped away from me and barreled through the militia men. His footsteps rang loudly on the metal staircase.

"Kelly, you'll take care of Chloe, won't you?" Shaw beseeched.

Kelly replied with a single nod.

Marshall Greer led the six of us back to our vehicles. We stayed silent the entire two hour walk back. Brandon walked ahead of us, followed by Shaw and Gareth. Fang, Ophelia, and I brought up the rear.

Brandon slammed his door shut when he got in the Shelby. Chloe's absence was stifling. He carefully schooled his features into an emotionless mask. I didn't know what to say, so I remained quiet. When we got onto the highway, the Shelby's engine roared to life as Brandon shifted into the highest gear and slammed his foot on the accelerator. Our surroundings whipped by in a blur. I gripped my seat so tight my knuckles turned white.

I couldn't take the silence anymore. I had to say something. "Brandon, I'm sorry—"

"Don't."

"You couldn't make her stay."

"I said I don't want to talk about it."

"But it's not your fault!"

"Sable, just shut up, for God's sake!"

As was typical of me, I only made things worse. I hugged my knees to my chest, which was uncomfortable to do with a seatbelt on, and rested my head on my knees. I stared out the window. I knew he was just lashing out because he was upset, but the irrational part of me was mad at him for doing it.

When we got off the highway, Brandon looked at me and sighed. "Look, I didn't mean to yell at you earlier."

"It's fine," I snapped. I still wouldn't look at him. He touched the back of my head and ran his fingers through my hair. I swatted his hand away and threw a glare at him before quickly turning my attention back out the window. He sighed again, more disgruntled this time, and parked the car. "What are you doing?"

"I have to wait for Shaw to catch up to us. We were going 120 miles per hour."

"*You* were speeding. I was sitting here," I replied icily.

"Sable. Look at me." I didn't budge. "Sable, please look at me."

I still didn't turn around, so he got out of the car. He stood on my side of the vehicle with his back to me. A plume of smoke rose from his head. Suddenly, the fact that he was smoking irritated me. I got out of the car and stalked over to him after slamming my door shut.

"So it makes you feel better to inhale carcinogens, but you can't talk to me about it?" I demanded.

After exhaling a puff of smoke he replied, "I'm not one for sharing my feelings."

The statement caused a sharp pain twist through my chest, leaving me breathless. Weren't we close enough for him to talk to me about it? Then again, it wasn't like we were a couple or anything. That thought only made me feel worse. "Whatever."

As I started walking away, he grabbed my arm and whirled me around to face him. "Where the hell are you going?"

"Away." I didn't know where I was headed. I hadn't thought that far ahead.

"Sable…" He pulled me close to him and pressed his lips to mine.

I wormed my hands in between our bodies and pushed him away. He let go of me and I stepped back from him.

"That's not going to make you feel better. Kissing me won't make Chloe come back." I wasn't expecting those pearls of wisdom to sound so bitter. His face crumpled for a split second before he regained control of his emotions and lit another cigarette. Then, blessedly, Shaw's Jeep pulled up.

XVII

I didn't have the energy to go to sleep. A week had gone by since we left Canada and landed back in the middle of the Atlantic Ocean near New England. Shaw instructed us to train for ten hours every day in case we had problems with the D.A.O. Fang trained Gareth, who proved to be a quick learner. Ophelia and I helped each other and sometimes Fang would instruct the three of us like we were his miniature class. Brandon trained on his own with intense and angry energy. Shaw had to replace one of the punching bags that Brandon hacked apart with a sword.

Brandon. I was so conflicted about how to feel toward him! Part of my heart bled for him. The only link he had to his biological family had left him. The loss of Chloe cut him deep. He kept to himself and increased his cigarette use from a few here and there to a pack and a half a day. His cooking suffered, too.

Breakfast usually consisted of burnt toast and rubbery scrambled eggs. Lunch and dinner were items he could whip up in five minutes or less. And he wouldn't talk to me anymore. That part pissed me off. One little refusal of a kiss and I get left out in the cold? Then my heart deflated again as I reminded myself yet again that we weren't an item. He owed me nothing, or I him. So why did his ignoring me make me feel like I had the stomach flu?

Ophelia was sound asleep. I decided to take solace above deck and watch the waves for a while. As quietly as I could, I pulled my fur trimmed black suede jacket out of the closet, slipped it on over my pajamas, slid on a pair of black wedge flip flops, and headed out. The air was frosty outside, and I was immediately grateful for my coat. I sat down at the edge of the deck and let my legs dangle over it. My arms rested on the rusty guard rail as I looked out at the dark water below.

The wind blew lazily across the water, creating tiny peaks in the ocean's surface. The full moon showed high overhead. It cast an orange glow on the water. I sighed as I let my mind wander.

Like every other time I'd let my mind drift off in the past week, I thought about the devastating events in Canada. Why was Chloe so eager to leave Shaw? What were the real motives of the D.A.O.? And why was Kelly so...I couldn't quite put my finger on what was off about him. At the time, I'd been so concerned with Brandon that I didn't give much thought to Kelly's zombie-like behavior.

More and more questions circled in my brain. I didn't have an answer for any of them. Frustrated, I lay back on the deck and rubbed my eyes. Then my mind settled on examining my relationship with Brandon.

We didn't talk a whole lot to begin with, then there were all those random moments of hot passion, and just when he starts letting me in a little bit, he freaks and freezes me out again. I still didn't think I was wrong for not letting him kiss me. I had more self-respect than to let myself be used as a vent of frustration.

The fact was that I empathized with Brandon about losing his family. While I never had siblings, I lost my parents when they committed me to the asylum. It was a pain so deep I couldn't describe it. Despite still being angry with him, I resolved myself to helping Brandon regain his family, no matter the cost. If he didn't have to lose Chloe, I wouldn't let him.

As fate would have it, I heard the click of Brandon's lighter. He stood at the stern of the ship, one hand in his pocket, the other holding his now-lit cigarette. I screwed up my courage and walked over to him.

We stood in silence for a long while. When he finished his cigarette, he flicked the filter into the ocean and regarded me with a nod. I took a deep breath. "Brandon—"

A loud clang made me jump. Brandon and I whirled around and found Ophelia running toward us. We ran to her and met in the middle.

"Guys, you have to come down to Shaw's office right now!" Her eyes were wild, panic stained her words. Without waiting to see if we followed her, she turned on her heel and ran back the way she'd come. Brandon and I glanced at each other and hurried after her.

When we got to Shaw's office, everyone was crowded around a small portable television that was on Shaw's desk. A "breaking news" banner scrolled across the top of the screen. The newscaster wore a grave expression on her thin face as she read from a teleprompter.

"...I repeat, there is a new threat to our nation. These new terrorists, known by scientists as 'Diseased,' are a danger to our society at large. Now, to provide further information on this latest threat is special guest Doctor Kramer." The screen cut to the doctor, a middle aged man on the verge of being old enough to draw social security.

"Thank you for having me, Florence. The Diseased look just like any average person. They could be your neighbors, your children's teachers, be in your church congregation, or be a relative of yours. The sickness causes supernatural abilities of the mind. The manifestations of this could appear as someone being able to read your mind. They might move objects with just a thought.

"Some are able to cause large impressions in the earth by sheer force of will. This illness can only be transferred through reproduction and causes people to have supernatural abilities. Persons who do not currently have the illness cannot contract it, but it may be passed along to your unborn offspring. Take precautions during intercourse to prevent this and other sexually transmitted infections."

Shaw let out an exasperated sigh and turned off the television. The rest of us all sat in silence, staring blankly at each other.

Finally, Brandon spoke. "Isn't this going to create mass pandemonium?"

Shaw nodded. His lips were pressed into a hard line, his eyes narrowed.

"What will this mean for us?" I asked.

"It means we're not safe anymore. We're going to be hunted," Shaw answered.

Fang's brow crumpled in confusion. "Weren't we already being hunted?"

"To an extent, but now everyone will be looking instead of just the people in high places, although this news release will make them more motivated to find us first." Shaw clasped his hands behind his back and paced back and forth; six steps, turn, six steps, turn.

"What do we do now?" Gareth piped up.

"Depends on how this goes. If people chalk it up to scare tactics, we stay on our toes, but we stay in the shadows. If the humans get violent, we'll have to fight. I sure as hell am not going down without a fight. We'll just have to keep an eye on the news."

Shaw stopped pacing and sighed. He scrubbed a hand down his face as he continued. "It probably won't be easy now, but try and get some rest. We're going to have to have some group combat training tomorrow. You know how to fight individually, but you'll need to know how to operate as a co-hesive unit."

Murmurs of acknowledgement sounded from the rest of us as we dispersed. I followed closely after Brandon. When he started gaining ground on the others who left before him, I touched his elbow and he paused.

"Brandon, I need to talk to you, please. It's urgent."

He turned to look at me, his hard eyes softening when they fell on my face. He nodded and kept walking. I followed him back up to the deck and toward the stern of the ship. When he decided we were far enough away from everyone else, he turned to face me again.

"Brandon I—"

"I have to go find Chloe. I have to make sure she's safe. The government won't take care of her. And if I can convince that traitorous bastard Kelly to come back, it's all the better. I shouldn't have let her walk away—" His voice broke on the last few words.

His body that had just been as tight as a stretched rubber band became slack, as if all his bones had melted into nothing. He turned away from me then and stared out at the water.

"That's actually what I wanted to talk to you about. I think you should go be with Chloe if that's what will make you happy. I shouldn't have told you not to go." I stared at my feet, embarrassment coloring my cheeks. As if that was his reason for staying. Me, his non-girlfriend. Was I really simultaneously that conceited and that pathetic? I saw his feet pivot again. His index finger caught under my chin. I let him guide my eyes to meet his.

"I didn't want to join the D.A.O. I should've fought harder for her to come back with us. I let her down." He still wore that crestfallen expression. It made my chest constrict. I reached up and placed my palm on his cheek, cradling his face.

He put his hand on top of mine and sighed. Then he bent down and pressed his lips to the hollow of my throat. My pulse leaped.

"I'll go with you to find her."

"No. Absolutely not. This is going to be dangerous, and I can't risk you being there." He took a step back and crossed his arms over his chest just as I anchored my hands to my hips.

"So, what, I'm just going to get in your way?"

"Quite frankly, yes."

I felt myself pale and silently thanked God it was dark outside so he wouldn't notice. True, I wasn't as skilled as Brandon, but I could definitely hold my own. "Like hell I will! You're not going to get rid of me, Brandon Harper. I'm going and that's that."

Brandon spluttered some incoherent words in protest, but at last, he let out a ragged exhalation of frustration. "Fine. We'll leave tonight. When Ophelia's sleeping, pack some clothes and meet me back here. I'm going to get weapons."

Before I could say anything more, he stalked away from me. Okay, so he wasn't happy I was going, but I was still going. Score one for me.

When I got to our room, Ophelia was in bed, reading a book. I pretended to be tired and lay down in my bed with my

back to her. After an agonizing amount of time, finally, Ophelia turned out the light. I waited ten more minutes to ensure she
was soundly sleeping before I raided the closet. I slung my zip
up hoodie, a few shirts, a few skirts and a couple pairs of pants
into a duffel bag, and slid my knee high, black patent-leather
platform boots on my feet.

Before I shoved my notebook into my duffel bag, I
scrawled a note for Ophelia:

Don't worry, we're fine and we'll be back soon. ♥

Brandon paced back and forth as I opened the door to the
deck. When he heard the soft squeak of the hinges, his head
whipped around and his eyes locked on me.

"Took you long enough," he muttered as he took my duffel bag from me.

I just rolled my eyes in response.

He slung the duffel bag over his shoulder and behind his
back and started down the rusted ladder on the side of the ship.
I followed after him, slipping a few times in my clunky boots.
Brandon cursed under his breath every time I slipped.

At the bottom of the ladder, he jumped into the waiting
speed boat below. I hesitated when it was my turn. I wasn't
confident in my ability to make a graceful landing.

"Come on," he called up to me.

"I am," I lied.

"We don't have until Christmas."

"I said I'm coming." My feet stayed cemented to the ladder rung.

A few tense minutes went by, but I couldn't make myself
jump. Finally, Brandon sighed and called up to me, "I'll catch
you. Come on."

"What if you don't?"

His arms were outstretched. He looked like a prince waiting to catch his princess that had just jumped out of the tower's window—without the look of love in his eyes.

I swallowed the lump in my throat and flung myself down to him. Somehow, I managed to land in his arms. He stumbled backwards a bit, but he didn't collapse, which was the main concern for me.

"Thanks," I mumbled.

He nodded once, but kept me pressed to his chest. I stared into his eyes, searching for some hint of emotion. He kept his breathing even, but his heart raced. Was he nervous about leaving like this?

"You can, um, put me down now," I whispered.

"Right," he said as he hastily dropped me to my feet.

Thankfully, I didn't topple over. I threw a glare at him, but it was fruitless because his back was turned to me. He untied the rope that tethered the speed boat to the ship.

"How exactly did you come by this, anyhow?"

"We have this on board all the time. I just had some of the crew help me get it into the water." He moved around the small vessel hurriedly, stowing away our duffel bags and preparing to set sail.

"The crew?"

"Well, yeah. Shaw hired them when he decided to live on the *Kandis Amelia* full time. You don't think that ship runs itself, do you?"

The truth was, I'd never thought about it before. "I've never seen any of the crew."

"They keep to themselves, mostly. I mean, we all do some maintenance around the ship, but primarily, it's the crew."

Before I had time to respond, the boat's engine roared to life. Brandon yelled something at me, but his voice was drowned out by the engine. The boat took off and I landed on my back. He must've told me to hang on. Thankfully, he didn't pay me any attention as I righted myself.

I made my way over to him and shouted so he could hear me. "Where are we going?"

"The D.A.O. is a government outfit, right? So I figure we'll start in D.C. and get some answers, then move on to wherever that leads us," he shouted back.

So, we were on a wild goose chase. Awesome.

About an hour passed and effects of sleep deprivation started to settle in. I wondered how it was that Brandon managed to stay so focused. Adrenaline, probably.

Beneath deck there was a small living area, with a dinette, a propane stove, a mini fridge, and a bathroom the size of one on an airplane. Beyond that was a room with an air mattress with a blanket and our duffel bags. I stifled a yawn as I walked over to Brandon.

"Hey, I'm going to bed. You should think about getting some sleep, too."

He cut the engine and dropped anchor. He must've been more tired than he appeared. I went below deck and he followed behind me. "You can take the bedroom."

It was sweet of him to be so chivalrous. "Then where will you sleep?"

"I'll sleep on the dinette bench."

I frowned. "That can't be very comfortable."

"I'll manage."

"You sure?"

He nodded, so I waved goodnight to him and went into the bedroom. A curtain served as the door, and I closed it.

Thankfully, I was already in my pajamas since I'd had to wear them to not rouse Ophelia's suspicions. I kicked off my boots and lay down on the mattress. Even though it was cold, the blanket was warm. But I couldn't escape the gnawing guilt of Brandon sleeping on the narrow bench. I got up off the mattress and padded to the curtain door. I peered around the edge of it. Brandon squirmed, trying to get comfortable. I frowned and made a decision.

"Brandon?"

"Is something wrong?"

"Yes. Will you come look at something for me?"

He rolled his eyes and scrubbed a hand down his face as he rose from the dinette bench. "What is it?"

I grabbed his hand and gently pulled on it as I sat back on the mattress. He looked totally perplexed, but he followed suit. "Sable, what—"

"Stay here with me."

"What?" His eyes grew wide and a blush spread over his cheeks. His sudden vulnerability made my heart stutter.

"Please." I stared into his eyes and squeezed his hand.

Behind those troubled eyes, he fought an internal battle. I couldn't help myself as my gaze dipped lower. He'd taken off his shirt to sleep, so he was just in his jeans. His body was hard with subtle musculature, just the edges defined.

Then I noticed his gaze lower from my face, too, just slightly. "I'll sleep on the floor."

Tendrils of fire licked inside my stomach. "You don't have to do that."

He brushed a few stray locks of hair behind my ear. "Sable…"

I couldn't resist him anymore. Something inside of me snapped, and before I could examine what I was doing, my lips were pressed to his, my palms flattened on his chest. He tensed for just a moment, then relaxed into me as his arms wound around my waist.

My hands explored the planes of his stomach and his back, my fingertips memorizing the cut of his muscles, the slope of his shoulders. His hands wandered from my waist, exploring me, too. Then his fingers slipped beneath the hem of my shirt and his frigid fingertips brushed my scorching skin. I fisted my hands in hair and kissed his throat. He pulled me closer to him, fitting our bodies together so there was no space between us. I sucked in a sharp breath. Gently, oh so gently, he cupped my face in his hands and moved me so I looked into his eyes.

"Baby doll, as much as it pains me to say this, and believe me, it does, we really need to get some sleep."

Baby doll? I liked the sound of that. He moved to stand, but I pulled on his hand and he stopped.

"Stay here with me. Please, Brandon," I begged, chewing on my bottom lip.

He sighed. "I hate when you say please."

"Why?"

"Because I can't say no."

Then he wrapped his arms around me and laid us down on the mattress. Despite the crazy mission we'd just embarked on and the fact that we had no clue where we were going or what we were doing, it was worth it to have this moment. I curled into his side and laid my head on his chest. His even breathing lulled me to sleep.

XVIII

Brandon's stirring caused me to wake up. He was trying to gently move my head off of his chest, but he wasn't the most graceful about it. I couldn't help but giggle. His body tensed at the sound, but he relaxed when he looked at my face.

"I didn't mean to wake you up," he said, smiling sheepishly.

"It's fine."

I yawned and stretched my arms, legs, and back. He waited until I was finished and I sat up before he moved.

"We've got to head out. It won't be too smart for us to sit for very long."

"Do we even have a plan?" My stomach got queasy when I thought about just how unprepared we were. Aside from some weapons, our hand to hand combat training, and our supernatural abilities, we were completely unprepared. This would be where Gareth's tracking ability or Ophelia's future seeing ability would come in handy. Too bad we couldn't utilize those.

He grinned as he rifled through his duffel bag. "We'll wing it."

Despite myself, I chuckled. I knew we'd have to play things by ear to a certain extent, but we needed some sort of direction. He pulled a pair of light-washed, wide-legged jeans and a black tank top out of his duffel bag. "I'll go change in the bathroom so you can have some space."

"Thanks," I replied as he walked off to the bathroom. I grabbed a charcoal, long-sleeved mini dress out of my duffel bag. How was that at all practical? As I pawed through the contents of my bag, I realized that I should've been more selective of the clothing I grabbed instead of just shoving the first few outfits hanging in the closet into the bag. I sighed and settled on the mini dress. Thankfully, I remembered to bring my comb. My hair was a tangled rat's nest.

After I was dressed and properly groomed, I joined Brandon above deck. The shoreline was visible off in the distance. Instead of fighting to make my voice heard over the engine, I placed my hand on his forearm and gently squeezed. He offered me a quick glance and a nod.

Then he really focused on me. His eyes swept from my booted feet up to my eyes, pausing in certain places for just a moment, causing me to blush.

"You um…that dress is…you look really nice," he stammered.

My cheeks heated further as I mumbled out a thank you. "So—back to that plan we need to make?"

"Right. So I'm thinking we need to make a scene. Then they'll come after us. If the D.A.O. gets their hands on us, Chloe and Kelly are sure to be with them. I'm sure we'll be able to convince someone to let us talk to them, even if we have to force them. When they come to talk to us, we'll kidnap them and bring them back with us."

"You've thought this out more than I realized," I muttered. Despite the assuredness in his voice, bile rose in the back of my throat. It reminded me too much of being in the asylum.

"You don't trust me." A statement, not a question.

"It's not that," I protested. He arched an eyebrow and crossed his arms over his chest. I sighed. "I'd rather not get into it, okay?"

He shrugged, but he didn't press me for details, thankfully. I sat down at the front of the boat and let the ocean spray cool my heated skin. I thought about how we would make a spectacle of ourselves. Fire would probably be more eye-catching than electricity. Then again, if we used both, we'd draw more attention. Especially if we made a spectacle of ourselves at night.

No matter how much I tried to calm my mind, I couldn't stop thinking about what would happen if the capture didn't go well. After all, the D.A.O. had offered us a place with them and we'd turned it down. What was going to make them so willing to cooperate with us now? Unless they were just collecting Diseased to make an army.

The thought smacked into me like a ton of bricks. They *were* collecting Diseased to make an army. What for, though? Who were they fighting? And if they were with the government, did that mean the Diseased with them would be killing others of their own kind or used as a different kind of soldier than what the armed forces currently used?

The thought made the bile come back to my throat again. Maybe being welcomed with open arms wasn't what we should worry about. Escaping the D.A.O. was sure to be the bigger challenge.

"Sable, are you okay? You look a little green." Brandon's eyebrows knit together, a concerned expression on his face.

"Yeah, yeah, just a little sea sickness is all," I lied.

"Okay." He let it go, but I guessed that he knew I wasn't being truthful.

As the day wore on and the growling in my stomach became more persistent, I began to regret not packing any food. I also felt bad for needing Brandon to drive the boat all day. I'd never driven one, and I didn't want to take a chance on wrecking our only mode of transportation. The sun had almost completely vanished beyond the horizon when we finally made landfall. I helped Brandon secure the boat to the public dock before we went to retrieve the weapons from our duffel bags.

When I first met Brandon, I'd assumed he wore loose fitting clothing as a personal style choice. I learned now that he did this to effectively conceal an alarming number of weapons on his person. After the first ten, I lost count of how many knives and daggers he had strapped to his body. To complete his horde of weaponry, he shoved a pistol into each of his front pockets. I stared at him in wonder as he put his T-shirt back on without piercing his flesh or tearing the fabric to ribbons. Then he began studying me.

I stood stark still as he unzipped my boots and strapped a knife to each of my calves. I assumed he put them there as a means of easy access. Since I wore a short form fitting dress, I didn't really have anywhere to hide weapons like he did. And I wasn't going to remove my clothes to get at them, either.

Then he wrapped a leather whip around my right forearm and wrist. It would have made a better fashion statement as a belt, but I didn't think it would stay secured there, so I left it.

I came out of my musings to find Brandon's eyes cast downward. He held a dagger in his hand, turning it over and over. His eyes darted between my face and my feet, never hesitating on one spot for too long. Swallowing hard, he knelt down and fixed the dagger into a holster. Timidly, he brushed his fingertips against the hem of my skirt. In a raspy voice, he asked, "May I?"

My mouth went instantly dry as I started nibbling on my bottom lip. My muscles tensed, almost painfully. It took great effort to offer him a stiff nod. I was almost surprised my neck didn't snap from the movement. Slowly, oh so slowly, he lifted my skirt to reveal my left thigh, stopping before my underwear would be visible.

Thankfully, I was already standing with my feet apart, because I didn't know how I would have mustered up the compulsion to move a millimeter. The leather holster felt like ice against my burning hot skin. A blush heated my cheeks as his fingertips accidentally brushed against my inner thigh while he buckled the holster in place.

Goose bumps broke out over my skin. I held my breath as he lowered my skirt back to the proper position. He studied the concealed weapon. I guessed it was hidden well enough since he didn't adjust it.

When he turned his back, my hand flew to my mouth, stifling the heavy exhalation bursting from my lips.

As we stepped onto the dock, my stomach growled painfully. I wrapped my arms around my waist, embarrassed by the sound.

Brandon chuckled at me. "Hungry?"

Sheepishly, I nodded. "I wish I had some cash so we could get something to eat."

"It just so happens that I have some money. Would you like to have dinner with me?"

I couldn't help but giggle a little. "Was I supposed to eat by myself, or..."

"Or?"

"Were you asking me out on a date?"

"Isn't that why you wore that dress?"

"That didn't answer my question."

He answered so quietly that I almost didn't hear him. "Yes."

"Well, then, let's go find some food." I took his hand and laced our fingers together. Now I appreciated packing this dress.

I'd never been on a date. Sure, I'd had a few boyfriends before, but nothing serious. The closest I got to going out on a date was when I liked a guy on my high school's football team. He asked me to come watch him play at an away game. I don't think he thought I'd actually go, because upon my arrival, he was making out with a cheerleader. I shoved the memory from my mind before it had a chance to taint my current lighthearted mood.

We walked a few blocks before stumbling upon a seaside diner which, naturally, specialized in seafood. The small space was decorated with kitschy fisherman décor. A large fishing net, draped over a stuffed and mounted marlin, was offset by a clipper ship's wheel on the opposite wall.

Even the windows, which were made to look like portholes, tied into the décor theme. The bench seats and seat cushions were upholstered with navy blue vinyl. Most of the seats had small holes or rips in the fabric. The waitress behind the counter held a finger up, indicating she'd be right with us.

"Hello, welcome to Dee's Diner. There's two of you today?" If she was older than Brandon or I, it couldn't have been by much. Her dark blonde hair was fastened into low pigtails by her ears.

A splash of freckles dotted her nose and cheekbones, adding to her youthful appearance. She wore black slacks and shoes with a cornflower blue, button-up short-sleeved shirt that complimented her large blue eyes.

We followed her to a booth. Brandon waited for me to sit before he sat across from me. After he sat, the waitress continued with her speech. "My name's Katie and I'll be taking care of you today. Can I get you something to drink?"

Brandon looked at me, waiting for me to order first. "I'll just have water."

"I'll have a Coke or Pepsi, whatever you have," Brandon answered.

Katie offered us a wide smile before handing us menus and bustling away to get our drinks. We cracked open the menus and I scanned the contents. What were you supposed to eat on a date? I decided the safest route would be a salad.

"Are you guys ready to order?" Katie asked as she set our drinks in front of us.

"I'll have a grilled shrimp Caesar salad," I answered as I handed her my menu.

"And for you?" she asked Brandon as she scribbled my order down on her notepad.

"I'll have a cup of lobster bisque and the scallop crostini."

After she finished scribbling his choices and taking his menu, Katie informed us she'd put our order in right away and hurried off to do so. Brandon and I sat in awkward silence for a few minutes. He was the first to speak.

"So...you come here often?" He scrubbed his hand down the back of his head. A nervous chuckle escaped him.

I laughed, too, but mine was from amusement. "Why yes, yes I do. The grilled cheese is exquisite," I grinned.

This time, he genuinely laughed. "What is it with you and grilled cheese?"

"I don't know." I shrugged. "Maybe it just conjures up happy childhood memories."

That part was true. From the time I was little, I remembered there being no better feeling than when my mother placed a plate of muenster cheese melted between two slices of buttery pan fried sourdough bread, the sandwich cut once down the center, making two triangle shaped halves.

My mother always baked her own bread. We never bought sandwich bread from the store. I would peel the crust off the sandwich, waiting for the cheese to cool a little, and save it for last. The crust was the best part. Then I'd take a bite and see how long I could pull the melted strings of cheese. My mother always served my favorite treat with a glass of raspberry flavored Italian soda.

"Sable?"

I blinked. "Yes?"

Brandon's grin widened as he rested his chin on his fist. "You look so cute when you're lost in thought."

"Thanks," I mumbled. My cheeks heated. I concentrated on drinking my water.

His gaze was honed on me like a laser. Doing my best to push my embarrassment down, I met his eyes. He studied my face with a smirk playing on his lips. "I can see why she likes you."

"What?"

"Well, I'll have to admit that it's weird to have similar tastes in girls as your sister."

I choked on the water I was drinking. Brandon did his best to hide a snort, but it wasn't hidden well enough. My eyes grew large as I gaped at him.

"I thought—isn't Chloe—I mean—Isn't she in love with Kelly?" I stammered.

"She's just really close to him. They're good friends, have been ever since he ended up at Shaw's ship. I think they're soul mates, really, just not romantically. The only person closer to her than Kelly is me."

With that admission, his face fell a little. Although my head was still spinning from the bomb he dropped about Chloe being attracted to me, my heart broke for him. I knew the loss of his sister was devastating, but I could never imagine how deep his love for her was or how badly their separation wounded him.

Brandon's hand laid flat on the table. I put mine on top of his. It was the only comforting gesture I could think of. There weren't any words to properly console him. He spread his fingers apart, lacing mine together with his.

"Sable..." His eyes locked on mine. Moisture lingered in them, making his icy blue irises look like melting ice. They took my breath away. I nodded for him to continue. "I just wanted to tell you that—"

"Shrimp Caesar," Katie said, placing the salad in front of me.

Brandon released my hand and leaned back against the bench seat.

"Thank you." I had to work at making my tone polite.

She didn't seem to notice the undercurrent of aggravation in my voice as she merely smiled at me. "Crostini and lobster bisque." She placed a plate with scallop adorned toast and a cup of creamy soup in front of Brandon. "Is there anything else I can get you right now, or are you doing okay?"

"We're fine, thanks," he answered.

"Enjoy!" Katie hurried away to attend to her other tables.

"Brandon, what were you going to say?" I asked as I popped a bite of shrimp and romaine lettuce in my mouth. While it wasn't bad, I thought it would taste better if Brandon had made it.

"Don't worry about it now, just enjoy your salad." He stirred his soup and looked off into the distance, his eyes not focusing on anything in particular.

We ate the rest of our meals in silence. Katie checked on us twice before bringing us the bill. Brandon left some cash on the table and we left Dee's Diner.

When we stepped outside, a thick fog had settled over the streets. As goose bumps broke out over my skin, I wished I'd thought to grab a pair of wool stockings. We walked to the center of town, which wasn't too far from the diner. Little shops dotted the main street, with colonial style houses dispersed among them.

The lack of kitschy gift shops made me think this wasn't a tourist hot spot. The glow of the street lights was marred by the fog, leaving an eerie light cascading on the occupants of the block.

I grabbed Brandon, who was walking two steps ahead of me, by the arm. He stopped.

"So where is it that we're supposed to make a spectacle of ourselves?"

He sighed. "Here's as good a place as any, I guess."

I doubted that, but I didn't question him. "What did you have in mind?"

"I hadn't thought that far ahead, to be honest."

He looked down at me then, and we were held in each other's gazes. His fingertips traced the line of my jaw, skimming across the apples of my cheeks. Then one of his hands locked onto my neck while the other anchored on the small of my back.

His lips brushed against mine, and I wrapped my arms around his waist. The cold steel of his weapons bit through the thin fabric of his shirt, chilling my hands. I was careful not to grip him too hard in fear of hurting him—or me—with one of those weapons.

He deepened the kiss and his grip on my neck tightened. His arm slung low around my hips as he pulled me closer to him, leaving no space between us. Heat crackled beneath my skin, fueling my intensity. Brandon responded with his own sense of intensity, and the heat grew. His hand left my neck and fisted in my hair. Needing to grip onto something, I grabbed his shoulders. My fingernails bit into his flesh and he groaned.

"Oh my God!" a woman shrieked. The realization that others were watching us stirred up my embarrassment and I leaped back from him. His eyes grew wide and he gasped. A pang of guilt flared in my chest. I didn't want him to think I was ashamed of kissing him in front of others. But wasn't that why I jumped back? No, I decided. I didn't want anyone seeing him that way but me. Man, was I getting possessive!

"I don't think we have to worry about that spectacle anymore," he whispered.

"I'm not sure a hot make out session counts as the type of spectacle we were aiming for," I retorted.

He shook his head, the action stiff. "Sable, look at your hands."

"There's nothing wrong with my—" As I held my hands up to examine them, I realized why the woman screamed and why Brandon's shocked expression was still glued on his face. Bright green flames licked across my skin. I looked myself up and down.

The flames were everywhere. Even my hair was on fire, but nothing burned. It was like a soft aura of fire. My eyes frantically darted over Brandon, making sure he wasn't burned.

Everything about him was intact. Then the accusations of the growing crowd around us began assaulting my ears.

"Is she a witch?" a child asked.

"She's one of those Diseased, like they talked about on the news," a man said.

"The boy must be, too. Look, he's unharmed," another man noted.

"What do we do with them?" a woman inquired.

All the overlapping conversations buzzed in my head like angry hornets trapped in a mason jar. I resisted the urge to press my hands tightly over my ears. In slow movements, Brandon made his way over to stand beside me. I was vaguely aware of some of the men loading and cocking their hunting rifles.

"Now we fight," Brandon murmured.

Then a blast of electric currents shattered the streetlights, casting a harsh bluish white light in their wake. Screams and cries of fear rang out into the night. Gunshots exploded above the chaos. I stood stunned in the middle of it all, watching everything as if it happened in slow motion.

"Sable!"

Brandon's voice sounded very far away, even though he stood right in front of me. He got farther and farther away from me as my vision tunneled in on his panic-stricken face, then it faded to black all together. All the while, I burned. It was for him, I realized. Burning from the inside out until everything was gone.

XIX

Don't move," Brandon whispered to me. "Keep your eyes closed and your breathing slow and even if you can."

Trying my best to keep the immediate sense of panic, welling up in me, out of my voice, I whispered back, "How did you know I woke up?"

"You tensed."

I could picture the smirk on his face. I fought to keep the look of unconsciousness on my face. The searing pain in my hip didn't help any.

Slowly, I flexed my fingers and squeezed my hands into fists. The resistance against my biceps told me that I was tied back to back with Brandon. We sat on a cold cement floor. Goosebumps covered the exposed skin on my thighs. I bit the inside of my cheek to keep from gasping in horrified shock. Someone might have seen up my skirt.

The cold steel on my calf eased my fear about that, though. I noticed that the weapons strapped to Brandon's back were missing. The hard planes of muscle and his spine mashed up against mine. Hardness meeting softness. Really, it was an inopportune time to imagine that contrast with our chests pressed together. A warm feeling spread through my abdomen as a mental image of us kissing popped into my head.

"Stay still," he hissed at me.

I flushed. I tried making my muscles as loose as possible, like a rag doll. Weren't unconscious people supposed to be like dead weight?

The click of tumblers disengaging in a lock made my blood run cold. Now we'd be faced with our captors. Brandon tensed, his spine becoming painfully rigid and cutting into my back. The ropes binding us together bit against my arms and torso. I held back a wince as I heard the door swing open. Soft thudding footsteps rang off the floor.

When the thudding stopped, a lighter clicked. An inhale and an exhale sounded. Cigar smoke wafted to my nostrils. I schooled my face to keep it blank. But I really wanted to wrinkle my nose in disgust.

I didn't mind so much when Brandon smoked, mainly because whenever he did, we were in a wide open area and he never blew the smoke in my face. This person had no qualms of concentrating that odor and forcing me to inhale it.

Callused fingertips brushed against my cheek. Mind numbing fear was all that kept me from shrinking away from the touch. A gravelly chuckle rumbled low in the smoker's throat.

He moved his hand down the side of my neck, pausing for just a moment to twist a few strands of my hair between his fingers, then resumed his descent to my collarbone, dropping lower—

"I swear to God if you touch her anywhere near where her undergarments cover her, I will make you die slowly by my hand," Brandon growled.

How did he know where the man touched me? I must've tensed again. If I tensed, that must mean—

"I believe the girl is capable of expressing her discomfort if she feels it," the gravelly voice said casually. This man had definitely been smoking for quite some time.

"How is she to defend herself if she's unconscious?"

"Young man, I am no stranger to telling lies, which means I know when one is being told to me. She's quite awake and aware of what's happening to her."

"Then you know I speak the truth about killing you if you touch her."

The man chuckled again. "Indeed."

Since there was no denying I was awake anymore, I opened my eyes, which settled on the man's face. I gasped as I registered how close his face was to mine. It was too intimate, but I couldn't back away, so I just blinked instead. His tanned skin had a weathered texture to it. Deep brown eyes burned in their sockets, watching me study what little of him I could see. His thick black hair looked like a wavy helmet on his round head.

Full lips parted into a wicked grin comprised of crooked bottom teeth and straight top ones, all of which were stained brown around their edges from years of smoking. The acrid stench of cigar smoke hung like a toxic aura around him.

"How are you feeling, little Phoenix?" he purred to me.

A shiver raked up my spine, sending a lancing pain through my hip. I gritted my teeth together to keep from showing any discomfort.

He looked at my hip anyhow and clucked his tongue disapprovingly. "I was hoping that would heal faster. At least the bullet was removed."

I felt the blood drain from my face and my eyes grow wide. I was shot in the hip? That explained the passing out, I guessed. My fingers twitched, trying to move to my hip to assess the damage. The ropes tied around Brandon and me prevented that, though. The man watched me with curiosity-filled eyes.

I squirmed. "Brandon, what happened?"

"What happened is that our undercover agents witnessed you lighting up like a brilliant green torch," the man answered. "The video is utterly stunning, I must say. Anyhow, one of those small town hicks shot you out of fear before we could attempt any type of crowd control. Luckily, the bullet merely grazed your skin and missed your bones. Quite remarkable, really, considering your lack of body fat—"

"That's enough," Brandon growled.

My fingers strained to find Brandon's without any luck. "Er, thanks, mister…"

"The name's Ivan Goldbrook," he obliged. "You may address me as Commander Goldbrook."

"Are you with the D.A.O.?" I asked.

"You're quite perceptive, little Phoenix."

The pet name irritated me, but I wasn't sure I wanted him knowing my real name. Then again, I was sure the D.A.O. had paperwork on us, so the fear was probably moot. "Why are we tied up?"

"Your little electricity wielding friend is actually quite volatile. I'm afraid the only way we had to restrain him in all ways necessary was to bind you to him. His fear of electrocuting you came quite in handy."

Commander Goldbrook stood then. I took in the rest of him. His large frame was boxy and stocky, but he definitely wasn't taller than me. He might've even been shorter. He wore a plum colored suit with thin white pinstripes, making me think he looked like a giant rectangular grape.

"Well, now that my friend sees that I'm perfectly un-harmed, and surely he will need to support my weight for me if I stand, disabling him from being volatile, would you please untie us?"

Even if I could stand on my own, I would pretend like I couldn't so we could do some investigating. Commander Goldbrook scratched his barely visible chin with a thick finger, considering my proposal. After a few tense moments, he sighed.

"I will agree to it. But be warned. If he attempts any act of violence, he will be exterminated on sight."

Brandon gave a curt nod. His spine was so rigid, I thought it might pierce through his skin and stab me in the back of the head. Commander Goldbrook took a knife from inside his suit coat and cut through the ropes. I sat in place, not daring to move without Brandon's aid.

He stood and popped some of his joints. I didn't turn around to watch him stretch. Then he moved to stand in front of me. He held his hands out to me and I took them. I put the majority of my weight on my good leg and stood as slowly as I could. As soon as my weight distributed through my injured hip, I hissed in pain.

I'd been planning to play up the injury so Commander Goldbrook found me less of a threat. Turned out, I didn't need to. It hurt like a bitch.

Just as my knees gave out, Brandon swept me up into his arms, careful of my gunshot wound. His gaze remained fixed on my hip, worry lines creasing the corners of his eyes and his forehead. Commander Goldbrook regarded us with a perplexed expression.

Then he nodded at Brandon and stepped around us to the door. I took in the room for the first time as we left it. Everything but the door was made of grey cement and there were no windows. The room was solely lit by fluorescent lamps. The metal door was painted battleship grey. As we left, the only thing in the room was the wheat colored rope that had been cut off of us and a pool of blood from my gunshot wound.

As much as I just wanted to bury my head in Brandon's chest, I forced myself to take in our surroundings. It seemed like we'd been locked in an unused storage closet. The rest of the space was painted in neutral beige tones and had a darker beige Berber carpeting. It could've passed for a doctor's office. Some people had their office doors open, and each office had small touches of personal flair to them, but nothing too distinguishing or outlandish. In each open office we passed, I saw a desk with a computer and stacks of paperwork on it, a desk chair, two padded chairs sitting on the opposite side of the desk, and filing cabinets.

None of them had windows. After a few twists and turns, we ended up at the door to a conference room. A long table that could easily seat forty people was in its center, a row of metal chairs with black plastic seats and back rests lined each side. A projector screen hung behind the head of the table. At the opposite end of the table was a cart with a projector and a lap top computer sitting on it.

This room also had the same beige décor as the rest of the building, including no windows.

Most of the seats at the table were filled. Many of the occupants were dressed in various military uniforms, while others were dressed in black power suits. Two chairs sitting next to one another were empty at the head of the table. Commander Goldbrook extended his arm, indicating the seats were for Brandon and me. Sitting opposite us were Chloe and Kelly.

As Brandon settled me into a chair opposite Chloe, I studied her face and Kelly's, each in turn. They both wore the same blank expression with glassy eyes that didn't seem to fixate on anything. The image unnerved me. They looked like zombies.

Brandon settled into the seat next to me and did his best to ignore his sister. I sensed his inner turmoil, but there was no time—or privacy—for me to try soothing his raw nerves. Commander Goldbrook took his seat at the head of the table. As I glanced down at the row of people, I recognized some of the faces from our run in with the D.A.O. in Canada. Captain Marsh was among them.

I noticed that the Diseased in this meeting wore all black, but not suits like the nonmilitary agents of the D.A.O. wore. The outfits hugged their bodies like wet suits. I counted fourteen Diseased including Brandon and myself. We were all seated nearest to Commander Goldbrook. I wondered if it was because he prized his supernatural soldiers or if it was because if they tried to escape they would have a more difficult time fighting the military members who sat closest to the sole door. The same zombie like state Chloe and Kelly were in seemed to possess the other Diseased, too.

My stomach twisted into a tighter knot with every dazed expression I took in. I grabbed Brandon's hand and squeezed it tighter and tighter until my knuckles threatened to rip through my skin. I chewed on my bottom lip. His eyes flicked over to me as Commander Goldbrook started speaking.

"My colleagues, thank you for joining me in this meeting. We have two potential new recruits with us this evening, a Phoenix and a Charger." At that, he indicated Brandon and me respectively.

Maybe I'd mistaken "Phoenix" as a pet name, and it was actually a label that defined my fire wielding ability.

"I'm proud to announce that our battalion of Diseased is almost complete" he continued. "It would be nice to have the

Shield, Seeker, and Omniscient with us, but there is still time to collect them.

"Our presentation to the Attorney General is imminent. This means we must all be in top form. Now, we all remember what we need to do, yes? I'll leave it up to our new recruits' previous allies to explain our presentation to them. The continuation of our research hinges on the success of this presentation. Now, Captain Fuller, if you'll escort the Diseased to their training area so our new recruits can become acquainted with the others and learn their role in the upcoming meeting?"

A tall, slender woman, with dark blonde hair pulled into a tight bun on the nape of her neck and sharp blue eyes, stood from her chair and nodded. The Diseased stood after her. She waited until Brandon gathered me out of my chair to open the door and exit through it. The Diseased followed her single file out of the board room. As the door snapped shut behind Kelly, who was the only person behind Brandon and me, Commander Goldbrook started speaking again.

Captain Fuller led us back the way we'd come, past the closet prison, to the opposite side of the building. The training room was similar to the one on Shaw's ship, but without the weaponry. The space was a wide open cube with wrestling mats littering the floor.

A young potted tree stood in the center of the room. As I assessed the other Diseased, I noticed more of them were men than women, and all of them were younger than thirty. Captain Fuller stood at the head of the room with a clip board in her hand. One by one, she called up the Diseased to display their skills.

Each Diseased had a different ability from the ones I'd seen before, and each had their own label. When Kelly was called, his label was Mover. He used his telekinesis ability to move one of the wrestling mats from one end of the room to the other with great speed, slowing it down just before it crashed into the wall. The mat gracefully descended back to the ground and landed with a soft thud.

"Phoenix and Charger, I'll have the both of you demonstrate before the Leech does," Captain Fuller said.

Brandon carried me to the center of the room to stand between the rest of the Diseased and Captain Fuller. The only Diseased still needing to demonstrate besides Brandon and me was Chloe. Why was she being called a Leech? She manipulated water.

Brandon set me on my feet. He quickly shot a jolt of electricity to one of the overhead fluorescent lights, making it short out and spark. Before my knees had time to give out again from the searing pain in my hip, he scooped me back into his arms. For my demonstration, I held my hand out and made a spiraling column of flames shoot out of my palm.

When the others looked sufficiently satisfied, I snapped my hand closed, extinguishing the spectacle. As Brandon and I took our place back in line, Chloe walked to the center of the room.

She was the reason for the tree. After plucking a leaf from it, it withered and crumbled in her fingers. Then she placed her palms flat on the tree. In a matter of minutes, the tree dried and splintered. The leaves fell to the floor, all dried and twisted and brown.

When she finished, her skin and her hair had a healthy glow to them. That was why she had so much trouble controlling water. She wasn't meant to use the water: she was supposed to suck the water out of everything else.

Brandon inhaled sharply, but no one seemed to notice except me. His hands gripped me so tight I was sure I'd have bruises. I looked up at his face, which was pinched looking and pallid. His mouth was set into a hard line as his hard as diamonds gaze zeroed in on Captain Fuller. She jotted notes down on her clip board before addressing the Diseased.

"You've all done very well, including the new recruits. You may return to your barracks, except for the Charger, the Phoenix, the Leech, and the Mover. The four of you will follow me to the infirmary."

"Captain Fuller, I request to accompany you to the infirmary as well," said the girl who stepped forward. Captain Fuller referred to her as Venom. She was the same height as Chloe, with the perfect balance of curves and musculature. Her mocha colored skin was flawless and her pin-straight black tresses fell to the small of her back.

Her hair was shaved on the sides, making a free flowing Mohawk. Her honey colored eyes stared out behind long black lashes, her pouty lips turned down slightly at the corners as she waited for an answer.

"Very well."

The statement was clipped. After the other Diseased made their exit, the five of us followed after Captain Fuller to the infirmary. As we walked, Brandon kept his eyes trained on Chloe. She walked in front of us, behind Venom. They both had the same stride. I imagined if I looked back at Kelly, who marched behind us, his gait would be very similar to theirs, if not exactly the same.

I cringed inside at the thought of becoming an automaton like the rest of the Diseased here.

I said a silent prayer in my head as we marched along. *Gareth or Ophelia, if you can hear me, if you're looking for us, we need your help. So do the rest of the Diseased here. But they want you, too, so be careful.* I wasn't at all confident they'd heard my plea. My stomach lurched as we stopped in front of the infirmary. I didn't want to be brainwashed like the rest of them. There was no other choice but to follow the others through the door. I sensed Brandon shared my feelings since he dragged his feet, causing Kelly to bump into him. How could I stop this from happening? I was completely powerless. I fought back tears of desperation as the door snapped closed behind us.

XX

C harger, set Phoenix down on the gurney," Captain Fuller instructed.

Brandon hesitated before complying with her demand. He stood next to me so our legs still touched. His eyes darted back and forth between Chloe and the door. I knew the look well enough to know he was trying to plan an escape attempt. If she were more lucid, Chloe would know it without a doubt, too, but in her current stupor, I couldn't be sure she'd recognize the wheels turning in her brother's head.

The door on the opposite side of the room swung open. A nurse dressed in white scrubs with pink hearts all over them entered the room backward, pulling a tray with medical instruments on it with her. My chest constricted and left me no air to gasp with.

My mouth opened and closed without a sound, like a fish struggling to catch its breath out of water. One sight of those medical instruments sent me straight into flashbacks of being in the Crazy Cannon Place.

The needles piercing my skin, the beeping of the monitors, the frigid air in the room. Their experiments couldn't possibly be as horrid as Doctor Pantiel's, right? Then again, the loss of your free will was a pretty terrifying concept to someone who still had theirs.

The nurse's mousy brown hair hung in a limp pony tail fastened on the crown of her head. Gray strands streaked through her temples. Like almost everyone else I'd seen at this facility, she was fit and trim.

Faint crow's feet and smile lines creased her fair skin. Brown eyes shone brightly behind light brown lashes. She wore no makeup except for pink lip gloss, which accented the natural pink tone in her cheeks. She smiled as she studied my face. "Please remove your dress."

My cheeks heated with embarrassment. Undressing in front of Brandon was one thing, but in front of Chloe and Kelly and these strangers? I shuddered. I squeaked, "Does everyone have to be in the room for this?"

"I'm not leaving you alone," Brandon said immediately.

"Does it not comfort you to be amongst friends?" Captain Fuller questioned.

I shook my head, not wanting to say anything potentially upsetting.

"Very well then. Mover, Leech, and Venom, you are to wait outside in the hallway until instructed otherwise."

"Yes, Captain," they answered in unison. Then they filed out the door.

When the door snapped shut, Captain Fuller turned her attention back to me. She crossed her arms over her chest and tapped her foot on the floor. I swallowed the lump in my throat and said a silent prayer as I removed my dress.

The gray fabric was marred by the large blood stain on my hip. Brandon swiveled in front of me so he blocked Captain Fuller's and the nurse's view. His hands slid expertly around my thigh, fingers working quickly to remove the dagger and its sheath. He stuffed them both up his sleeve as Captain Fuller cleared her throat: a subtle warning for him to move out of the way. Before complying, he left a quick peck on my forehead.

"Well, I suppose it's a good thing the sides of your underwear are barely there strips. It'll make it easier to stitch this wound up," the nurse muttered as she threaded a needle.

Before she sewed up the gunshot wound, she applied local anesthetic via injection near it. I chewed on my bottom lip through the whole process. Brandon's hand clasped my shoulder at the start of it.

"Captain Fuller, do we have anything else for her to wear?" The nurse shook her head in disgust as she tossed my dress in the trash. "I'd hate to send her back out in this blood stained thing." Then she busied herself with cleaning the instruments she'd used for the procedure, turning away from us.

"We'll see what Commander Goldbrook has to say about it." Captain Fuller spun on her heel and barked orders for the three in the hallway to return to the room.

I looked at Brandon, horrified. He cursed under his breath, removed his shirt, and thrust it at me. While I slipped in on—thank God it was almost long enough to be a dress on me—he stashed the dagger into the back pocket of his jeans. At the sound of the door latching closed, the nurse turned her attention back to us.

"Where's Captain Fuller?" she asked with mild curiosity in her voice.

"She's gone to inquire about a set of clothes for the Phoenix," Venom answered.

"Well then, I'll be back in a few minutes. There are other people I need to attend to." She bustled through the swinging door with her cart while she spoke.

We sat in tense silence for a few moments. Kelly, Chloe, and Venom stood as still as statues. My curiosity won out over my fear, so I asked, "Venom, what's your real name?"

Her head swiveled in my direction, but her gaze didn't quite meet mine. "Leilani Olsen."

"Leilani. That's a pretty name."

"It's Hawaiian."

"So why does Captain Fuller call you Venom?"

She sighed. "Most of the people around here do." Her smooth features crumpled in exhaustion as she pinched the bridge of her nose between her thumb and index finger. "My saliva is full of venom. A small amount in someone else's bloodstream makes them compliant to my will, but larger amounts of it will kill."

"So is that—is that why the other Diseased are—are like that?" I pointed a trembling finger towards Kelly and Chloe.

They stood frozen as if nothing was happening around them. Leilani nodded solemnly.

"Are you happy here?" Brandon asked suddenly.

"I don't have a choice." Acid filled her reply.

"That wasn't the question. Do you want out?"

She stared intensely at Brandon, who offered the same intensity in response. Finally, she gave a curt nod.

"If you control all the Diseased here, why not use them to help you get out of here?" he demanded.

"It's not that simple!" she hissed. Then she schooled her expression into a featureless mask. Captain Fuller came through the door a moment later.

"Commander Goldbrook has provided this for you to wear," she announced as she thrust a black piece of cloth toward me.

I took it in my fingertips as she released it. The fabric was sheer; reminding me of a slip like you'd wear under your dress.

"Um, could I have a minute to redress?"

Captain Fuller snapped her fingers and Leilani, Kelly, and Chloe followed her out the door.

I slid off the gurney and stood gingerly. Brandon's grip latched onto my waist. My nerves had me shaky everywhere, so I was glad for the support. I squeezed my eyes shut, took off Brandon's shirt, and slipped the sheath dress on over my head. Spaghetti straps held the dress up, and the skirt wasn't much shorter than my sweater dress was. My grey bra straps showed under the thin dress straps. It made me feel a little trashy. As if she'd been peering through an imaginary keyhole to see when I'd finished dressing, Captain Fuller opened the door.

"It's time for you two to report to your barracks. Mover will escort Charger to the male barracks and Phoenix will be shown to the female barracks by Venom and Leech," she instructed briskly.

Brandon scooped me up in his arms, careful not to touch my freshly stitched-up hip, then squared his shoulders. "I'm not letting her out of my sight."

"It is not permitted for men and women to share sleeping quarters."

"Then we'll sleep somewhere else. Either she stays with me in the men's barracks or I stay with her in female barracks. Or you could let us leave." The hair on my arms and the back of my neck stood up. Electricity was very close to the surface of Brandon's skin. If not for his immense self-control, he'd be a giant ball of electrical currents right now, and me along with him.

A muscle ticked beneath Captain Fuller's right eye as she considered Brandon's proposal. "You will stay with her in the female barracks. But be warned, Charger, that if there is any sort of sexual contact between you and a female, you will be eradicated immediately."

With that she spun on her heel and barked instructions to Leilani and Kelly. Brandon followed behind Leilani and Chloe marched behind us. As we wove through the maze of hallways towards the female barracks, I whispered in Brandon's ear, "Thanks for staying with me."

He shrugged. "Less chance of us turning into soulless soldiers if we do."

The female barracks were every bit as depressing as the basement of the Crazy Cannon Place. Thin cots littered the floor, most occupied with young Diseased women. The floors, walls, and ceiling were made of unpainted cement. Whispers filled the rectangular space as the women took in the sight of Brandon.

"Hush," Leilani commanded softly.

The whispers died as soon as the word left her lips. Chloe broke off from our miniature marching line and settled onto an empty cot. I wondered if the cots were specifically assigned to people or if you just lay down on the nearest empty one. Leilani stopped at a pair of empty cots and turned to face us.

"Charger, you will sleep on the floor next to Phoenix's cot. I will have my eye on you," she warned.

"Can he at least hold my hand?" I asked shyly. A desperate gnawing in my chest demanded I stay connected to him somehow.

"No."

"I bet if I was a girl I could," Brandon muttered.

"Not even then." Was that sadness in her voice?

Brandon laid me down gently on the cot. I rolled over on-to my side to make sure I wouldn't lay on my stitches. The anesthetic was starting to wear off and a dull ache throbbed through the wound. He lay down on the floor next to me on his back. He rested his head on his palms. I wanted to offer him my pillow, but I knew he wouldn't take it. I sighed and closed my eyes.

How were we ever going to get out of here? Brandon and I weren't left alone enough to talk over any kind of strategy. At least we'd managed to keep one of our weapons. I imagined he would sleep better in this place armed. As dutifully as he looked after me, I knew he ached to reach Chloe somehow. Every time his eyes fell on her, his muscles tensed. If I had a sister whose free will was stolen from her and I didn't know how to give it back to her, I would be a ball of stress, too.

As hard as I tried to fall asleep, unconsciousness wouldn't come to me. Deciding I wasn't going to be able to sleep, I opened my eyes and looked around. Women were sleeping on rows of cots as far as I could see.

Given that the room was still brightly lit by fluorescent lights, it wasn't difficult to do. The women whose features I could clearly make out all looked like they were about my age or just a little older. Was young adulthood the perfect age for brainwashing?

The thought of me being brainwashed made my nerves jump. I trained my gaze on Brandon's face to distract myself. That only made me feel worse.

He hadn't moved at all since falling asleep with his hands behind his head. His face was screwed up into a grimace. I imagined he was dreaming about Chloe, about how he couldn't save her.

My heart broke, watching his disturbed sleep.

"You're in love with him," Leilani said, making it an observation rather than a question.

"Shouldn't you be sleeping?" My eyes wouldn't leave his face.

"I've never been in love." Her voice was wistful.

That caught my attention. Fighting the urge to stroke his face or kiss his lips, I looked up at her. She lay stretched out on her side, her head propped up by her hand, watching me with a guarded expression.

"This is a first for me," I said. "How old are you, anyhow?"

"Seventeen."

"I'm sixteen. He's seventeen, too. Are most of the Diseased here teens?"

"Many of them are. Some are in their twenties."

"How did you end up here?"

"My family is very poor. The government offered them five thousand dollars for me. Because I was a freak, and because they were so desperate, they accepted the offer."

"Your family sold you?" I repeated, incredulous. I couldn't believe it. I mean, my parents threw me into a loony bin, sure, but they didn't exchange me for money. Had they?

"It's history now." The tears in her eyes betrayed her indifferent attitude.

I had the urge to hug her, but I stayed put. Could I afford to make friends here?

She wiped her eyes with the back of her free hand. "So how did you end up here?"

"I was kissing him," I said, indicating Brandon, "and I was consumed by flames. The townspeople flipped out and someone shot me. Now we're here."

A click of the lock made us both fall silent. Brandon bolted upright, his hand flying to the dagger in his jeans. A man entered the room.

He was dressed in all black and had salt and pepper hair tied into a pony tail at the nape of his neck.

His eyes locked with mine, and then he started moving toward me. Why did he seem so familiar?

As he held his finger up to his lips to tell us to stay silent, I couldn't help but gasp. "Roger?"

XXI

Leilani jumped to her feet and stood in an attack pose. "You know this man?"

"Yes, I do. He saved my life once," I answered.

Brandon and Leilani both regarded me skeptically. He sat up and looked at Roger, who was almost next to us now.

"Ophelia called in a favor, so here I am. I'm supposed to get you out of here. There're four of you, right?" Roger asked.

"Five," I corrected him.

"Well, we don't have much time. Where are the other two?"

"One's in this room and one's in the men's barracks, but I don't know where that is."

"They won't go willingly," Leilani informed him. "I'm controlling everyone on the same wave of thought. I can't break them off separately like that." She sighed as she slumped back down on her cot.

"You can't give them more mind control serum?" Brandon asked gently.

"I don't have any syringes or needles, so I'd have to…I'd have to kiss them both." Her cheeks darkened, making her look like she'd just been out in the sun on a warm day. The color looked good on her.

"I'm sure they'll forgive you when we're free," I encouraged.

Leilani twisted a piece of the hem of her shirt between her thumb and index finger.

"I don't mean to push you, Miss, but we do need to hurry," Roger pressed. "I'm not sure how much time we'll have before we're discovered or if we'll be apprehended."

She took a deep breath and nodded.

"Sable's injury will slow us down, too," Brandon muttered.

"What injury?" Roger asked.

I sighed. "I got shot in the hip."

Roger knelt next to me and placed his hand gently on top of the wound. I gritted my teeth and sucked in a breath at his touch. Brandon moved to knock Roger's hand out of the way, but Roger caught Brandon's arm and shoved it back. My hip heated, then the warmth concentrated itself, getting hotter and seeming to drain into my wound. The heat was white hot when it was just in my injury. I squeezed my eyes shut and chewed on my lip. A whimper escaped from my throat. I felt Brandon's hand cup my jaw, his thumb stroking gently across my cheek bone. Then the heat evaporated and the pain in my hip was gone. Roger removed his hand and sighed. Exhaustion darkened his features.

"How did you do that?" Brandon marveled.

"He's a Healer," Leilani observed. Roger nodded.

I stood slowly, making sure my body wouldn't betray me. Brandon wrapped his arm around my waist. I didn't need the support, but I wouldn't discourage his touch, not ever again.

"Leilani, you have to get Chloe. Do you want us to wait back here or do you want some uh…moral support?" I finished lamely.

"I can do it alone."

Leilani walked over to Chloe with squared shoulders. She knelt down next to Chloe's cot and shook her shoulder lightly. Chloe blinked her eyes open and stared dazedly at Leilani. Then Leilani bent her head down. Brandon cleared his throat and busied himself with checking my hip while Leilani kissed his sister. Then she whispered unintelligible words into Chloe's ear.

After a few tense moments, Chloe sat up stark straight. Her eyes scanned the room and locked on Brandon. She bolted over to him, careful not to disturb the sleeping women, and threw her arms around him, knocking me backward. Roger caught my fall. I was too relieved that Chloe was back to herself to care that she'd shoved me out of her way.

Brandon gathered his sister in his arms and held her close to him for a moment before holding her out at arm's length. His gaze raked over her like he hadn't seen her in a hundred years.

"Where's Kelly?" Chloe asked.

"We still have to go get him," Brandon answered.

We all turned to look at Leilani then. Seeming to understand that we needed her to find the men's barracks, she started toward the door. Roger walked behind her, followed by Chloe. Brandon wrapped his arm around my waist again, but his attention was clearly on his sister.

Every so often, she'd look over her shoulder at him. I'd never seen either of them smile so much.

Leilani led us through the labyrinth of beige hallways until we got to the men's barracks. She entered alone while the rest of us stood guard outside. I guessed it took about ten minutes or so for her to "wake up" Kelly, but it seemed like much longer. Every little noise made me jump. Brandon would squeeze my hip every time I jerked in surprise. I guess it was to remind me I had protection.

When Kelly emerged through the doorway, he and Chloe embraced. It wasn't quite the tender moment she and Brandon had, but it was pretty close. Leilani stood in the doorway, allowing the friends to rejoice in their reunion. Another wave of relief washed over me as I watched them.

There was life in their eyes again, real joy in their smiles, and quiet laughter. Kelly released Chloe and gave me a hug. I threw my arms around him and squeezed him tight. He and Brandon nodded at one another, a silent expression of relief and happiness.

"I hate to spoil the moment," Leilani said. "But I don't know how to get out of here. None of us Diseased know how. We're not allowed to wander too much, so that way we can't find it."

Roger winked. "I'll find the way out. I've left a trail behind."

I giggled. "Did you leave a trail of breadcrumbs?"

"Nothing quite so primitive. I've used a paint of sorts that can only be viewed under ultra violet light." While he explained, he pulled a flashlight the size of an ink pen out of his breast pocket. So that's why it looked like he was dragging his fingers against the walls, I thought.

He clicked the pen and a small spot of purple light the diameter of a quarter appeared on the wall. The light bobbed up and down as he searched for the paint. He breathed a sigh of relief when a bright white-violet line popped off the wall.

Almost as if we were all too nervous to even breathe, we followed the glow in silence. I silently thanked God these floors were carpeted and muffled the sounds of our footfalls.

As we neared the exit—Roger made a hand print on the escape door—a frigid wave of fear swept through me. Something felt wrong about the fact that we were escaping a government institution unscathed. Shouldn't there have been guards by the doors or something? Roger's power was to heal, not to harm, so he wouldn't have been able to hurt anyone. Although, if he was still a double agent, maybe they'd let him pass through willingly. I held my breath as Roger opened the door. The air was thin and still, but still seemed too thick and heavy to inhale. Suddenly, my head slammed into the ground.

I must've only been out a moment or two because when my vision cleared, it looked like a whole army was swarming in on us. Brandon stood directly in front of me, his body humming with electricity. A white hot ball crackled between his hands, waiting to be thrown at a target. Quickly, I scrambled to my feet.

I willed the flames to consume me. Starting from my core and spreading out to the top of my head and the tips of my fingers and toes, orange fire engulfed my skin. A few cries of panic and surprise sounded. Brandon released his lightning ball on a few soldiers trying to rush us. Kelly used his telekinesis to stop the bullets zooming toward us.

He caught most of them, but a few managed to graze Chloe and Leilani. Chloe and Brandon both cursed under their breaths and set into hand to hand combat.

"I could leech them," Chloe grunted as her booted foot landed heavily on a soldier's chest.

He flew backward and landed sprawled on the ground. Another soldier rushed her. Her foot connected with his chin. Quite a feat for someone so short.

"Wouldn't that kill them?" I cried as Brandon punched a guy, who came for me, in the stomach.

"Who the hell cares?" she protested as she fended off the latest attacker.

A group of men sauntered around Leilani before they started choking each other. She must've kissed them all. The thought made me shudder. Not that she'd kissed them all, but that her influence could have easily spelled the same fate for the rest of us. It still could.

"We won't kill them," Brandon decided.

Somehow, we managed to make slow but sure headway through the crowd of attackers. I joined in the fray, throwing flames at anyone getting too close to us. I figured out I could make a pathway for us to escape through. I moved closely behind Kelly. While he deterred the bullets, I made walls of fire to keep the soldiers back. The ones Kelly managed to miss peppered us both. At least Roger could patch up the bad injuries later.

Somehow we managed to reach a small truck with a capped bed. Roger jumped into the driver's seat while the rest of us clambered onto the bed. The engine roared to life. With a couple backfires from the exhaust, we lurched forward. The sound of bullets spraying the ground behind us perforated the growl of the engine. Flames shot out of the tailpipes.

"He must have NOS," Brandon said as he followed my gaze.

"Is anyone injured?" Kelly asked.

"We'll have to search for them when the sun rises," Brandon replied.

Since no one protested, I guessed no one had any serious injuries.

"Ladies, Brandon and I will keep watch. You sleep," Kelly instructed.

Leilani yawned. "We're in an enclosed truck. What could possibly happen?"

"You could use your 'influence' against us," Brandon suggested.

"Eventually, you're going to have to trust me."

"We'll see about that," he replied darkly.

I nestled against Brandon's chest, letting the sound of his breathing and his heartbeat fill my ears and lull me to sleep. Chloe laid her head on Kelly's thigh. He offered the other to Leilani. She declined and leaned against the rear window of the cab.

და

I blinked awake as sunlight streamed through the windows. Leilani had caved and taken Kelly up on his offer to use his leg as a pillow. She and Chloe faced one another. I imagined they would be stirring soon, too. Before I gave away that I was conscious, I took a moment to enjoy being wrapped in Brandon's arms. Somehow, it didn't matter what the situation was, only that it felt like home being in his arms like that.

As I sat up, I studied Brandon's and Kelly's faces. They both stared out at the barren landscape whizzing past us with bloodshot eyes. Then I scrutinized all our clothing. Everyone had tattered remains of what they'd worn before. The dagger Brandon took from me was visible through the rips in his sleeve. I wondered if having a weapon was like a security blanket to him. Then his lips pressed against my forehead. They were rough and cracked, but nothing could ever feel better against my skin.

"Good morning," I whispered. Kelly's head swiveled to me. He offered a slight wave and I returned it. I imagined he was trying not to jostle the sleeping girls more than the truck already was. "Where are we?"

"Texas," Brandon answered in a low voice.

"What?"

"Don't worry about the how. We stopped for gas once and Roger said we were going to California. He ran out of NOS, so we've probably got at least a couple of days left in this truck."

A groan escaped me. Brandon and Kelly chuckled. Leilani stirred at the sound. She sat up and rubbed the sleep from her eyes. Kelly kept his gaze fixed on Chloe.

Brandon laughed. "She sure is pretty when she's sleeping and not running her mouth."

"She's pretty the rest of the time, too," Leilani said softly.

I blinked my eyes in surprise as I watched her cheeks flush. Leilani liked Chloe. I mean, she *liked* Chloe. I knew because that was the way I stared at Brandon sometimes. My head snapped up to look at him. He and Kelly didn't seem to notice the way Leilani stared at Chloe. Boys were so oblivious!

The truck crawled to a stop at a remote gas station. Roger hopped out of the cab and walked into the general store. A few minutes later he returned with a paper sack. He set it next to him on the ground while he fixed the gas pump into its place in the truck. When the pump started filling up the gas tank, he picked the sack up and opened the tailgate of the truck. Chloe awoke to the creaking metal.

"Breakfast." Roger smiled as he rummaged through the sack. He pulled out a sticky bun with pecans wrapped in cellophane before he pushed the sack toward us.

Chloe grabbed it and started tossing out its contents: a pack of beef jerky, a bag of barbeque flavored potato chips, a box of custard filled chocolate frosted donuts, and a six pack of cola. She twisted a can of cola out of its plastic ring and tossed it to Roger. I grabbed the box of donuts and took one. While it wasn't a gourmet meal like Brandon's, I savored every sugary-sweet morsel as if it was. I hadn't eaten since the "date." Brandon tore into the beef jerky, which he shared with Chloe. Kelly settled on the potato chips and Leilani ate a donut.

We finished off the sustenance as Roger pulled the truck back onto the road. We girls convinced the guys to go to sleep. Surely three of us during the day were better lookouts than the two of them at night. Brandon sat between my legs and leaned his head against my chest, like I had with him. I wrapped an arm around his chest and he put his hands on top of mine. I ran my fingers through his hair, my nails gently grazing his scalp. His breathing settled into a slow even rhythm as he fell asleep.

Chloe rolled her eyes and let out an exasperated sigh as she watched us. "Do you really have to do that in front of everyone?"

"Well, at least I can tell you're back to normal," I muttered.

Leilani's brow crinkled in confusion as Chloe snorted haughtily.

"So when we get to California, what do we do?" Leilani asked.

She spoke with a soft accent that I couldn't place, but it added to her exotic features. I would've killed to have her bone structure and an ounce of her naturally golden tan.

"I don't know," Chloe confessed. Her face fell from its grimace of distaste to an expression of pensiveness.

"Roger said Ophelia told him to go there," I explained.

"Who is Ophelia?" An edge in Leilani's voice let on to the fact she didn't like being so uninformed. She might have the potential power to control us all, but she was at our mercy.

I shrugged. "She's in our, er, group. She sees the future."

"Just how many of you are there?"

"Do you think we should just be answering all her questions?" Chloe's expression was indifferent, but her words were razor sharp.

I smiled. "There's eight all together. You could make nine."

Chloe and Leilani both looked skeptical about the idea. I thought it was better to have her on our side instead of against us. We'd already seen the disastrous result that caused. "Look, you don't have to make a commitment right now or anything, it's just something to consider."

"Indeed," Leilani muttered.

The three of us stayed silent after that. I looked down at Brandon's face. It made my heart break a little. Even in sleep, his features were still screwed up by everything that had happened, and probably by the fear of what was to come after this. He couldn't even enjoy the fact that we'd gotten Chloe and Kelly back.

The hairs on the back of my neck stood up, making me think I was being watched. I jerked my head up as Chloe made a sound of disgust and snapped her head around to look in the opposite direction.

What the hell was her problem? The answer slammed into me like a ton of bricks. Brandon's voice floated through my mind. *'I'll have to admit that it's weird to have similar tastes in girls as your sister.'* A sort of strangled choking noise escaped my throat. Leilani and Chloe's gazes both locked on me. I offered them a weak smile, my cheeks heating with embarrassment. Without the offer of an explanation for the sound, they returned their attentions to staring out the windows.

Wait—Chloe was staring out the window. Leilani was staring at Chloe, though not in an obvious way. A fleeting glance at her would make you think she was staring out at the passing desert landscape. Upon closer inspection, though, she kept stealing little glances out of the corner of her eye at Chloe. I smiled to myself. I'd have to tell Brandon about it when we were alone. Not that that would be anytime soon. With a heavy sigh, I stared out at the landscape as it whizzed by. Different shades of brown and mountains in the distance blurred together to make it seem as if we were in a snow globe filled with sand instead of snow. A sign saying El Paso, Texas, was one hundred ten miles away was a green blip in all the beige.

XXII

S able, we're here." Kelly gently shook my shoulder. His smile was warm despite the tension lines that creased his brow and the corners of his eyes.

I hadn't realized just how much I missed that smile when he was gone. I smiled back at him and rubbed the sleep from my eyes.

As Kelly climbed out of the back of the truck, I took in the sights around me. Streetlights made orange bubbles of light along the pier. Everything else was dark. Waves breaking softly on the shore created a natural melody to break the stillness of the night.

Just beyond the glow of a streetlight stood a large congregation of people. Half of them I rode to California with. The other half I'd left behind in the Atlantic Ocean to find lost comrades. I broke into a sprint. I'd never run so fast in my life.

Fang scooped me up into his arms and squeezed me tight. "Don't you go running off like that again, Miss Sable!"

I sighed happily. "I missed you, too."

"Don't you ever scare me like that again!" Ophelia demanded as she sandwiched me between her and Fang.

I laughed and nodded. Soothing warmth spread through me. My skin glowed with an inner effervescence. Even though I was in a new place, I'd never felt so much at home as I did with Fang and Ophelia beside me.

My eyes strayed over to Brandon. He and Shaw had their heads bent together. I wondered if Brandon was debriefing Shaw on our impromptu mission. Kelly and Chloe joined Brandon and Shaw. Gareth wandered over to us. He offered me a nod of recognition.

I returned it with one of my own. Leilani stood off by herself. She kept a close watch on the two groups, but shifted her weight from one foot to the other. I loosed myself from Fang's hold and went over to her.

"Do you want to come meet everyone?" I smiled at her and offered her my hand. If we were going to get her to join us, we'd have to make her feel welcome. She studied my hand for a minute before she took it in hers.

I breathed a silent sigh of relief. We walked back over to Fang, Ophelia and Gareth. "Everyone, this is Leilani. She escaped with us. This is Ophelia, Gareth, and Fang, respectively."

"Pleasure," Leilani said brusquely.

"Likewise," Ophelia answered in the same manner.

Well, I couldn't expect everyone to warm up to her instantly.

"Leilani, Brandon tells me that you're able to bend others to your will with a single kiss." Shaw accepted this as fact. He trusted Brandon.

I was relieved that Shaw didn't think less of him for taking off like we did.

Leilani cast her eyes downward. "Yes, sir, I can." Was she ashamed of her ability or just what she did with it?

"Perhaps your skills may be of use. Be warned, however, that should you use your talent against any of us, you will be ostracized and left to fend for yourself. Will you agree to join us?"

"I will join you," she answered meekly.

"Very well. My name is Shaw. I trust you've been introduced to the others."

"Yes, sir."

"Sable, might I have a word with you?"

I nodded and followed Shaw a few paces away from the others. Ice surged through my veins, making my movements stiff. It was the same way I felt when I got called into the principal's office at my school—when I set the contents of the trash can on fire.

He stopped abruptly and turned on his heel to face me. I almost ran into him. I flashed him an apologetic smile as he crossed his arms over his chest. My stomach twisted into a knot. "What's happening, Shaw?"

"First of all, I want you to know that what you did was extremely stupid. You're not as proficient in your training as you believe you are."

"I never said I was—"

"Brandon's my best warrior. You could have cost me a great deal." Then he let out a long sigh and pinched the bridge of his nose between his thumb and index finger. "You could have cost me my son."

"I didn't mean any harm, I promise. I just knew that Brandon was going crazy without Chloe and I had to help him get her back."

"And by some miracle, you were successful. Don't be foolish enough to think that success will be repeated."

"I'm not that horrible in combat!"

"Like I said before, you're also not that excellent, but that wasn't what I was referring to. Come, let's rejoin the others and I'll explain."

Before I could comment, he pushed past me and strode back over to the others. Thankfully, Kelly was trying to include Leilani in the conversation.

Just before Shaw reached everyone else, Roger blocked his path. "I must leave, my friends. Hopefully we'll meet again someday."

"Thank you for returning the lost to us."

Shaw and Roger shook hands. With a smile to me, Roger turned away and headed for the truck. It was probably best that he left before Shaw spilled our new plan of attack. At least he could plead ignorance that way if he was still acting as a double agent, which I suspected he was.

The friendly conversation died at Shaw's arrival. I stood with the rest of the group by Kelly and Leilani. Tension filled the air as we anticipated what Shaw had to say.

"First, I would like to express how thankful I am to have Kelly and Chloe returned to us. I am also pleased that Gareth has decided to permanently join in and fight for us. I hope that Leilani will decide to align herself with us permanently, but that will come in time.

"As we made our way to the west coast, more and more media attention has been brought to the Diseased and what we're potentially capable of doing. Some programs have gone as far as offering rewards to people who turn us in to be studied. A large sum of money has also been promised to the Diseased who willingly turn themselves in for experimentation.

"This means we must be more vigilant than ever about concealing ourselves and training in case we need to defend ourselves. Ophelia, have you seen anything we should be concerned about?"

"Yes. At some point, the D.A.O. will come for us. There are some major abilities among us that are prized by the war leaders. The D.A.O. will not keep us safe, but will instead use us as instruments in battle or as a means of torturing prisoners of war, among the more sinister applications." The color in her face drained away as she spoke. Everyone stood stoic and disturbed.

"Where do we go from here?" Kelly asked.

Before anyone could answer, blue and red flashing lights and the blip of a siren perforated the otherwise tranquil atmosphere. A police car pulled onto the pier and stopped in front of our group. The officer shined his unreasonably bright flashlight on us. The glare of it made me squint.

"Break it up, folks, or I'll call in back up and you'll be arrested for loitering," he ordered. His voice boomed out of a bullhorn.

"We were just leaving," Shaw replied.

Shaw led the way down the pier. When the officer turned off the glaring flashlight, the sky seemed too dark. I blinked my eyes a few times in an attempt to adjust them more quickly. It did little good.

"Ophelia?" Gareth asked.

The rest of us stopped and turned to her. Her gaze was glassy and unfocused, the sign she was having a vision. When she snapped back to the present, she gasped and her eyes grew wide.

"What did you see?" Shaw demanded.

"There's so many of them…" Her voice was barely audible above the sound of the water lapping at the pier.

"Who is it?" Gareth asked gently.

"Roger made the call. He told them where we were. The D.A.O. is coming, and they're not even a day's time behind us."

Shaw, Brandon, and Leilani swore.

"Who the hell is he working for?" Chloe demanded.

"He's a double agent," Ophelia answered wearily.

"We don't have much time, then. Everyone, board the ship," Shaw instructed.

Our sense of urgency had everyone running down the pier to the dock at top speed. Shaw and Fang climbed the rusty ladder on the side of the *Kandis Amelia* first. Brandon and Kelly ushered the women up the ladder before scrambling up it themselves.

As the ship moved away from the dock, Brandon declared, "Everyone needs to get a good night's sleep. We start rigorous training in the morning. Chloe, show Leilani to her room."

Chloe nodded and grabbed Leilani by the arm. Everyone else followed suit and made their descent to the lower decks. Just before I reached the door, I felt a hand grab my forearm. I waited until the others were out of sight before I turned around.

Brandon was backlit by the moonlight. It cast a bright glow on his hair, making it look ashy. Tension locked his muscles, making his grip on my arm a little too tight to be comfortable. I looked up into his eyes. Faint tension lines creased the corners of them.

"What's wrong?" I asked.

Releasing my arm, he sighed. "I just wanted to say thank you for helping me rescue my sister."

"Of course."

"Well, I guess we should get some sleep, too."

"I guess."

Neither of us moved at all. I started chewing on my bottom lip, waiting to see when he would break his stare and head for the door to the stairwell. His arms wound around my waist and pulled me close to him. Suddenly, there was nothing I wanted more than to be in his arms, enveloped by him.

"Damn it, Brandon!" Chloe shrieked.

I groaned and let go of him. I was glad she was back safe and all, but...

Brandon grinned. "I'm coming."

Chloe made a growling noise as she whirled around and stomped down the stairs. When she was out of sight, Brandon looked back at me, his dazzling grin still playing on his lips. "You better get some rest, too. Goodnight, Sable."

"Goodnight, Brandon," I whispered as he descended down the metal staircase leading to the decks below.

I sank down on the deck, hugging my knees to my chest as I stared out at the dark water. The ship moved almost noiselessly through the night. It felt like forever since I'd been in this place, when really it had only been a few days. Would life always be like this now? Would we always be on the run? I closed my eyes and sighed as I thought it over.

I released the hold on my legs and held one palm upturned toward the night sky. A flame appeared there, dancing listlessly in the minimal breeze. *I wish that one day, we can all be safe.* I blew the flame out like a birthday candle and opened my eyes. Sprawling out on the deck, I fell asleep gazing at the stars.

About the Author

Marissa Bauder is a longtime lover of fiction, particularly young adult fiction. She took the leap from reading the books she loves to writing a story she loves, and it wound up being a book! When she's not reading or writing, Bauder can be found playing Hide-and-Go-Seek with her daughter, snuggling up with one of her cats, or enjoying some reality television. Bauder lives with her family in southeast Ohio.